DADDY B

BEARS OF FOREST HEIGHTS: BOOK 1

Roxie Ray

© 2021

Disclaimer

Contents

Prologue - Zoey

The wind whipped my hair up around my face, but it felt wonderful. In fact, everything felt good. Graduation was only a week ago, but it seemed like it had already been years. I sat in my room on the window sill, letting the breeze flow in. The summer was a blank slate, and decisions had to be made. At the moment, I kind of felt like I was on the top of a mountain, the whole world below me, any direction I wanted to go. No doubt the direction I wanted would not be what my parents approved of.

My sister died ten years ago. She'd been the wild one, partying, boyfriends, in trouble in school. She'd been out with three friends, and they'd all gotten drunk and decided to drive home. The car had wrapped around a tree. All three of them passed away that night.

That had been one of the worst mornings of my entire life. Mom and Dad had cried like I'd never seen them before. My sister was never coming home again. It was awful.

For the decade since, I'd been an absolute angel, terrified that I would worry my parents or add to their heartache. Great grades, nice friends, extra-curricular activities, the whole nine yards. I was sure they felt great about how my life was going.

I, however, felt suffocated. I needed a release, something exciting! For once in my life, I wanted to be *bad*. I'd never had a drink; I'd never done more than kiss a boy. Shoot, I'd never even done silly things like skinny dipping. This summer would be different. I had three months before college, and I was going to live, damn it!

"Zoey?" Mother called.

I sighed. She knew I preferred to go by Zo. I'd tried to tell her for over four years now.

"Yeah?" I called. It wasn't the moment for that argument.

"Aunt Patty is on the phone. She has a really cool question for you."

I frowned as I swung my legs around and walked to the hallway. Mom was there with her cell phone, smiling down at it. She handed it to me as I gave her a suspicious look. Why did I feel a scheme afoot?

"Aunt Patty?" I asked.

"Hey there, Zo, how're you doing?" she asked.

It was nice to hear her voice. Scheme or not, I'd always loved Aunt Patty. She was the coolest relative I had, and she always remembered I liked going by Zo.

"I'm good. What's up?" I asked.

"Well, I was talking to my little sister there, and I mentioned that it had been way too long since I'd seen you. And, well, I wondered if you wanted to have a little adventure before you go off to college. Do you want to come up to Idaho and hang with your crazy aunt for a few months?"

My jaw dropped, and I looked at my mom, an amazed smile spreading on my face. "Are you guys for real?"

Mom nodded as Aunt Patty said, "Well, hell yeah, I am." She chuckled. "Does that mean you're coming?"

It was like a dream come true. A whole summer, thousands of miles away from anyone who knew me? Other than Aunt Patty. I could be whoever I wanted, do what I wanted, and no one I knew would ever find out.

I couldn't stop my voice from raising an octave. "Uh, yeah! That sounds amazing! Oh my gosh, I'm so excited."

After only a little cajoling that night, my dad agreed too, and three days later, I was on a plane for the first time in my life.

The ride was the most exhilarating thing ever. I'd managed to talk my mom into not going with me for the trip up. She'd wanted to go with me on the flight and spend a day or two there before flying back. I'd told her how much I wanted to experience traveling by myself, and to my surprise, she'd relented. My *immense* surprise.

Happy as I'd ever been, I sat for hours looking out the window watching the entire world flow by under me. I'd figured I would nap for a while, but that never happened. I was way too excited to be on my first semi-adult adventure.

The plane landed in Boise just after lunch, and I felt like a full-blown adult getting my carry-on and making my way off the plane. Walking down the terminal, I saw Aunt Patty waving to me like a lunatic. I laughed and jogged over to give her a hug.

"Holy crap! You're really here!" She yanked me into her arms and hugged me tight.

"Looks like it," I said into her hair. "It's good to see you too."

We went to baggage claim and got my stuff. I was having a hard time focusing as I watched everyone around me, wondering where they were going, where they'd been. It was kind of crazy how many people were coming to and going from Idaho. I'd sort of pictured a tiny little airport with potato farms as far as the eye could see.

Not so. Boise was crazy big. It was no Charlotte by any means, but it was a much larger city than I'd imagined.

We ate lunch at a neat little pizza place near the airport, and then made the forty-five-minute drive to Forest Heights. The urban environment quickly faded to the more rural setting I'd originally imagined. There were a lot more trees and mountains than I'd thought there would be. Again, my imagination had painted Idaho as flat potato country. Nothing like I'd expected.

We did pass a few farms, and one midsized town before I saw the sign welcoming us to Forest Heights. It was the cutest little town I'd ever seen. It even had the classic downtown main street area. I wasn't sure what kind of trouble I could get into here, but I was definitely going to try.

"We're going to stop by the store before we get to the house. I want to stock up the fridge and pantry with stuff you like. Sound good?" Patty asked.

I nodded as we turned into a small market on the far end of Main Street. I got out and went in with Patty. It was definitely small—I doubted they would have many of the things I was used to from the mega-marts back home. Though, I was pleasantly surprised to see hummus and organic guacamole. I walked around the store with a hand-held basket while Patty pushed around a shopping cart.

As I stood in front of several shelves of crackers, deciding which kind I wanted, someone behind me asked, "Oh...my...God! Where did you get those shoes?"

I turned and found myself looking at a pretty girl about my age, maybe a little older, with thick blonde hair pulled high into a ponytail. Her bright blue gaze was locked on my sandals.

Shifting from one foot to another, I tried not to be too awkward. "Oh, hey. Uh, yeah, I got them online actually. They're super comfortable."

"They look great on you! My name's Kim, by the way. Are you new? I've never seen you around before." She beamed as she waited for me to figure out how to form words.

"I'm Zoey, I go by Zo. I'm actually from South Carolina. I'm up here visiting my aunt for the summer." That was a lot of information. Had it been too much? "And I'm eighteen."

"Holy shit! That's awesome. Do you live by the beach?" Kim asked, her eyes locked on mine now. "And I'm nineteen!"

I laughed. Everyone asked that. "No, more like central South Carolina." I shrugged. "I've been to the beach a bunch, though."

"Ugh, I've never been. Trying to save up for a trip to Jamaica for my twenty-first birthday though. Still a few years away. It'll be great! Nude beaches? Rum? Hot dudes with abs? Can't fucking wait!" She had a serious potty mouth, which was great. I did, too.

I laughed. I liked this girl already. I asked, "Do you want to hang out sometime?"

Kim nodded vigorously. "Hell yeah, let's do it! There's actually a party I'm going to tonight if you wanna come."

A party? Like a real party? I had never gone to a real party. The closest I'd been to were birthday parties. Even for teenagers, they'd been super tame, daytime affairs.

"Absolutely," I said.

I gave her my number and my aunt's address. "Text me when you're on the way," I said excitedly. Kim agreed and we parted ways with big smiles.

Unlike my parents, Patty actually seemed excited for me to go to the party and that I'd already made friends with someone.

"So, you don't mind if I go?" I asked.

She blew out a big breath. "Of course not. Have fun! I mean, my gosh, you're only young once. Just not *too* much fun, you know what I mean?"

"Okay, cool! Thanks!"

The rest of the day went by quickly as Aunt Patty showed me the house, where I'd be staying, and I settled in.

My nerves were absolutely shot all day. The time passed like a snail on downers, but finally, Kim pulled up. We got to know each other a little bit better on the ride. Compared favorite boy bands, foods, and hair dyes. Typical teenage girl stuff.

It was almost eight o'clock before Kim and I pulled up at what looked like a warehouse. A ton of cars were parked in the parking lot. So many that we had to find a spot in the grass with a dozen other cars. How many kids around here had their own vehicle? Kim did, but I'd assumed this would be a high school party.

I got out to the steady thump of music. That was when the butterflies started. My stomach made little flips as we turned toward the imposing building.

"Let's go, girly!" Kim said and sashayed past me. She'd chosen a tube top and the shortest shorts I'd ever seen in my life. My bathing suits had more fabric than she was wearing. I followed her in, feeling a little self-conscious about how I'd dressed. It was a simple summer dress, and the sandals Kim had loved so much. I had no idea what proper attire was for something like this.

I walked in and immediately realized I was in over my head. Not high school, not at all. The air was thick with the smell of beer, whiskey, cigarettes, and what I thought must've been marijuana. No one looked younger than twenty-five, at least other than Kim and me. Most of the men looked old enough to be my dad, with most all of them wearing leather jackets.

Some had full leather ensembles, pants, boots, everything. Someone bumped into me, and before I fell, I grabbed a nearby table, trying my best not to lose my balance. I turned and looked wide-eyed at a woman wearing knee-high leather boots, a leather thong...and nothing else. Her breasts swung freely, and she laughed as she bent over a table and quickly snorted a line of white powder up her nose. I glanced down at the woman's breasts and saw a strange design tattooed just above her collarbone almost on her neck. It looked like an animal with an open mouth. Several men near her had the same symbol stitched on their jackets or tattooed on their arms or chests. It looked almost like a bear.

Oh, crap! Where am I?

I grabbed Kim's arm and stayed close to her as she made her way to a group of the youngest-looking people in the room.

I whispered in her ear, but I had to talk kind of loud over the music. "Who are these people? Why do they have that symbol on their clothes and stuff?"

Kim looked at me confused, and I watched realization dawn on her. She laughed and shook her head.

"Oh, whoops!" She laughed. "I didn't tell you! This is a shifter party. A bunch of people here are bear shifters."

My eyes bulged when she told me. I'd never actually met a shifter. Not in real life, anyway. There was a wolf clan compound about three hours from where I lived back home. And a girl I knew in school had sworn up and down her aunt dated a lion shifter when she was younger, but no one believed her. My butterflies exploded into full-blown nausea.

"It's fine," Kim said. "Here, this will make you feel better."

She shoved her hand into a fifty-gallon drum of ice and beer and pulled a bottle of Corona out. I blinked rapidly as she slapped it into my hand and pulled me along to introduce me to some people she knew. I didn't even slightly hear their names. Instead I glanced around while twisting the top off the beer. I'd never had a drink before, and it felt wrong, but I lifted the bottle up to my lips anyway with my stomach clenching from nervousness and a healthy dose of fear. This was it. This was me being rebellious and daring. Maybe a little too much so. After all, I didn't really know Kim. Had she brought me somewhere dangerous?

The liquid hit my lips. Okay. Weird. Not bad, but not good either. Kind of sweet, but also sort of musty. Almost like wet, yeasty bread. I didn't let the taste stop me, though. I tilted my head back and drained half the bottle in four quick gulps. The taste was worse that way, and I decided to just sip on it for a little while as I followed Kim around the building. She mingled with people she knew or met new friends. After about twenty minutes, I started feeling much calmer and less stressed.

Maybe the beer was having an effect. I definitely wasn't as self-conscious as I had been walking in.

After starting my second beer, I got the feeling I was being watched, almost like fingers brushing my neck. I turned around, scanning the room, trying to see if I was crazy, and that's when I spotted him. Leaned against the wall on the far side of the building, his gaze locked on me. He was too far away for me to see his eye color, but he was drilling straight into my soul with that look. And holy freaking crap. He was gorgeous.

And then he noticed me noticing him, before he pushed away from the wall and started toward me. *Holy crap.* The closer he got, the better I could see his face. He was older than me, somewhere between twenty-five and thirty

maybe? As he got closer, everyone hurried to get

out of his way. He didn't have to excuse himself at

all. It was like the seas parted before him. Seeing

the patch sewn on his leather jacket, I tried not to

gasp. He was a shifter too. This man, this *shifter,*

walked right up to me, incredibly close. Way

inside my personal bubble.

As he leaned his face close to my ear to talk,

I smelled him. Sweat, motor oil, mint toothpaste,

and soap. It was a pleasant combination for some

reason.

His lips almost brushed my ear as he said,

"Never seen you around before. I'm Rhett, but call

me Grizz."

I turned my head, both to put a little distance between us and to get a better look at him. His black hair was long and tied back. There was thin stubble across his face, not long enough to look sloppy, but just enough to look good.

I tried to answer as calmly as I could, "Um...my...uh, my name is Zoey, but call me Zo."

He laughed at that, a beautiful, deep, masculine laugh. I smiled too, and against my wishes, my nipples went hard and started to ache as my cheeks went scarlet.

"Well, Zoey-goes-by-Zo. It's very nice to meet you. How old are you anyway? Did you just move here?" Grizz asked.

I shook my head rapidly. "No. Just visiting my aunt for the summer before college. I'm eighteen."

"Well, I'm very glad you're here. I love having something beautiful to look at," he said.

My cheek grew even hotter, and I wasn't sure I'd be able to continue breathing. He was flirting with me, I knew, but this was not like the way high school boys flirted. He was...aggressive. I had to admit I kind of liked it.

"So, um, what do you do?" I asked.

He shrugged and said, "A little of this, a little of that."

I smiled, feeling more comfortable. "That's pretty vague."

"I meant it to be," Grizz said and winked at me.

It went like that, between us, for almost an hour. The flirting was nice. Eventually, he put his hand on my lower back, and I put mine on his arm. Each time we touched, it was like electricity crackled in the air. Finally, Kim found me again. Her eyes went wide when she saw who I was talking to.

"Hey, Grizz," Kim said.

He only nodded to her and smiled.

Kim looked at me with narrowed eyes, like she was shocked I was talking to Grizz. "Hey, it's getting late. You ready to go?"

I wasn't, but knew I had to get home at a fairly decent hour. I'd only just gotten to Idaho. I couldn't stay out till dawn. As cool as Aunt Patty was, that would probably not be a great idea.

I looked at Grizz. "It was nice talking to you tonight."

He brushed his hair back and behind his ear. "Yup. So, how long are you staying in town? You said all summer, right?" Grizz asked.

I only nodded in response.

"You should come back and see me sometime. I'm here almost all the time."

I nodded again like an idiot, and said, "That would be really nice."

And I did keep going back. The first couple of times, it was a little weird. No party or other people hanging around. We would just sit and hang out. I met his brothers, Hutch and Reck. Hutch was a little bit of an ass, and Reck was just a kid, maybe twelve or thirteen. He seemed to be a handful.

It was apparent they were a rough bunch. I didn't ask, but it didn't take long for me to figure out that Grizz and Hutch were in some kind of gang. It didn't seem like they liked to talk about what they did. Those first few weeks, I learned that I liked vodka and orange juice, and I got drunk for the first time. Thankfully, Grizz called Kim to take me home that night. Again, Aunt Patty was super cool about it all. Telling me about the

time she and my mom had drunk half a bottle of

whiskey while my grandparents were out of town.

They'd puked for nearly the entire next day.

As embarrassing as that had been, Grizz had

never made fun of me or joked about it. He wasn't

like any man I'd ever met. He complimented me

often, made me feel wanted, desired. Being

around him made me feel sexy. And I had never

felt that way in my entire life.

On my third week in Forest Heights, Grizz

called me and asked me to come up to the

clubhouse for another party they were having.

"Tonight? Is it going to be like the one

where I met you?" I asked.

He grunted and laughed. "Probably."

I rolled my eyes. "Okay, sure. Why not?"

Kim and I got there just after nine. It was actually an even bigger party than the last one. Yelling and shouting greeted us from inside. I walked in and saw two of Grizz's gang were having a wrestling match in the middle of the room with everyone circled around them. It looked like a few people were exchanging money, betting on who they thought would win.

Kim went right for the circle, but I skirted the edge and found Grizz leaning against the makeshift bar. It was just a piece of plywood on top of two sawhorses, with bottles all across it. He turned and spotted me. Without a word, he grabbed a bottle of vodka and a jug of orange juice from a tub to his right.

"Should I make the girl her favorite drink?" he asked once he'd already started pouring.

I nodded and watched him make it. He didn't have his jacket on, and I could see the muscles in his forearms and biceps flex as he made the drink. I grew warm just being near him.

I'd had a thought, plenty of them, about what might happen tonight. It terrified me, but I felt like an asteroid caught in a planet's gravity. It felt inevitable. Inescapable. And I wasn't sure I wanted to escape.

We both had a couple of drinks and talked as we watched a few of the wrestling matches.

They all ended with laughs and backs being patted. It was all good-natured.

I had to hide my surprise when two of the girls in the crowd went for a match. They were both scantily clad to begin with, and quickly became mostly naked as they struggled against each other. The screaming and yelling got louder once nudity was involved. Grizz smirked as the last match was over and the music was turned up.

The wrestling floor turned into a dance floor.

After letting myself daydream about being pulled out onto the floor, I had to bite back laughter. I had never seen Grizz dance, and decided he probably wasn't the dancing type.

I was trying to think of something to say

when I felt his hand on my chin. Startled, I let him

turn my head, and before I knew what was

happening, he was kissing me.

His tongue darted into my mouth. Grizz

drew me closer, my breasts pressing into his

chest, heat radiating off of him. It was like leaning

against an oven. His hand moved from my chin to

the back of my head, gently running his fingers

through my hair.

I sighed and let myself relax into the kiss.

Opening my mouth, I let my tongue twine with his

as my heart beat out of my chest. His other hand

slid down and clutched my butt gently.

Too soon, he pulled away, looked me in the eye and said two words, "Follow me."

And I did. He took me by the hand and walked me up the stairs. At the end of a hallway, Grizz led me into his room. The sound of the lock on the door clicking made my nipples pucker again.

Grizz stalked across the room and kissed me again. This time it was deeper, hungrier. His hardness pressed through his pants, and I got excited knowing I was the one doing that to him.

He pulled away again, and I stifled a groan of disappointment.

"Are you a virgin?" he asked.

I nodded my head, my body shaking, nearly shivering in excitement and fear. Warmth spread between my legs, moving up my stomach. It was an ache I'd never felt before. Not this desperately, not with this much hunger.

"If you want to, we can. I promise I'll be gentle," Grizz said in a near pant.

I tried to speak but I couldn't; words wouldn't come. Instead, I nodded and quickly pulled my shirt over my head. The air hitting my naked skin made my nipples grow tighter and harder.

Grizz's gaze seemed to devour my breasts. He didn't speak either, just pulled his shirt off. The fine hair across his broad chest and down his rippling abs was a bit of a surprise. It made me want to drift my fingers through it, tickling him and letting his fuzz tickle me.

I'd heard shifters were all in amazing shape, but I didn't realize their bodies were nearly perfect.

I sat on the bed and pulled my shoes and pants off as quickly as I could, keeping my gaze on him the entire time. He kicked his boots off to the side and unbuckled his jeans as he walked toward me. I lay back on the bed, only my panties still on, fighting the urge to cover my breasts. So far the whole thing was exhilarating, but a little awkward.

Biting my lip was the only way I managed to stop myself from gasping and hyperventilating as

Grizz slid his pants and boxers down in one swift movement. My jaw fell open at the sight of his dick hanging between his legs, growing hard and beginning to rise. He was so big, I didn't know how he would fit in me.

I sucked in my stomach as Grizz bent over me and kissed me gently. It wasn't that I wanted to look skinny, but more of an instinctive reaction. I was so excited, but I didn't know what I was doing.

He brushed his hands across my breasts and nipples. I gasped, it felt so good. It made the spot between my legs clench, and I groaned. His manhood slid across my thigh as he straddled me. I'd never even touched one before. Against my leg, it was hard and surprisingly smooth and soft, like velvet. I couldn't stop my breathing now, my breath coming hard and fast. I had never been so nervous or horny in my life. All I wanted was for him to be inside me, but I was also scared. It might hurt.

Grizz looked me in the eyes and slid his hand down between my legs. I was wet. Damn, I didn't even know I could get that wet, and when his finger slid inside me, I dropped my head back. Clenching my eyes closed as his fingers slid deeper, I felt a moment of dull pain, but then pleasure returned. It was even better now, like I was fully open.

I whispered, "I want it. Oh, I want you. I'm

ready, I'm ready." But I wasn't sure I really was.

Grizz nodded and spread my legs. It wasn't

easy to relax, to let him see me exposed like that.

"You don't...You don't need a condom,

right?" I asked. One last bit of hesitation made me

ask.

He shook his head. "Shifters don't catch

disease, and we can't get humans pregnant. It's

okay."

I nodded and rubbed my hands against the

muscles of his chest as he pressed himself against

my sex. The thick bulge of his head rubbed against

that secret spot, and my body shuddered. I wasn't

breathing, holding my breath, waiting for the inevitable as I watched him move.

Then, with aching slowness, he slid inside me. He was so big, it felt like his entire body was sliding into me, filling me in a way I had never experienced. Before he was all the way in, my body rocked with the first orgasm of my life. Spasms of pleasure rolled over me, wave after wave, vibrating from between my legs.

I let out a loud groan. The world vanished for a moment as I came, colors exploding behind my eyes as I clenched around him. I opened my eyes and looked up at Grizz just as he finished filling me with himself. Then he began to move in and out slowly, gently, and again I came. I sat up and clutched at his back as my body shook and he grunted as his thrusting grew faster, hungrier.

I lost track of how many times I came, but by the time his shoulders grew tense and he shuddered within me, I was covered in sweat and felt like I'd run a marathon. It happened so fast, yet seemed to take my entire lifetime.

I held him there, clinging to my first lover as he recovered. And at that moment... I fell completely in love with Grizz.

The next several weeks were filled with lots of sex. *Lots* of it. I would hang out with Aunt Patty or Kim during the day. But nearly every night, I had Kim give me a ride up to the clubhouse. If I were honest, it was the best time of my life. Over that summer, Kim became the best friend I'd ever had. Aunt Patty and I grew closer than ever. I was also thinking, at the back of my mind, that I didn't even want to go back to South Carolina. I had everything here, friendship, family, a man I was in love with. I could visit Mom and Dad whenever. Maybe I could get into Boise State and just go to college up here. The thoughts got stronger the further into summer we got.

About ten days before I was supposed to fly back home, Kim and I sat in a little burger joint having lunch when I told her what she wanted to do.

She gave me a weird look. "Zo, I don't know how to say this but...I wouldn't get overly attached to Grizz. I mean, I'm sure it's fun. Every woman in and around Forest Heights would cut off their left tit to get that man in the sack. He's just not the type to settle down. He kind of has a reputation for bouncing around to different women. I just figured you were playing around too. I didn't think you were really falling for him."

I shook my head and said, "You don't understand. It's different with him. I know he loves me too."

Kim almost choked on her milkshake. "You love him? Zo, come on!" she said around her coughing. "This is just some summer fling. It's a great story you'll tell your sorority sisters or something. I mean, maybe even pull up some nice dirty memories in a few years."

"Kim, I..." I stopped. I didn't feel good all of a sudden. My stomach felt awful.

I took a deep breath, but could tell it wasn't going away. I needed a bathroom. I stood and ran to the back of the restaurant with Kim close at my heels. I got to the toilet just in time and emptied my stomach, heaving for several more minutes. Kim stood behind me, rubbing my back.

"Are you okay?" she asked.

I nodded and wiped my mouth with toilet paper. "It happened yesterday too. I thought I had a bug or something but then I felt better," I said.

"Zo, are you pregnant?" Kim gasped.

"What? No, I've only been with Grizz. Shifters can't get humans pregnant. Right?" I asked.

She nodded, "I mean, yeah. It's pretty common knowledge, but still. This looks like morning sickness. Let's just get a stick for you to piss on. They cost like three bucks, and it'll make me feel better."

I chuckled but agreed. We stopped off at the drugstore and grabbed a cheap and an expensive test, because Kim wanted to be a hundred percent sure. She seemed more nervous than I was. We took our bag and receipt and went straight to the bathroom in the store. I pulled down my pants and peed on both sticks. Kim set them on the sink and we waited.

A few minutes later, I asked Kim, "How long does it take?"

She grabbed both boxes and read for a few seconds, then looked at the tests. I watched her whole body freeze. She looked at the boxes again, then back at the tests. She turned and looked at me, panic and shock on her face.

"You are, like, a thousand percent sure Grizz is the only guy you've been with?" she asked.

I jumped up and looked at the tests. Both were positive. This wasn't possible.

Kim shook her hands, starting to freak out. "I mean, are you sure you didn't, like, I don't know, get super drunk and maybe...maybe someone took advantage—"

"No!" I cut her off. "Absolutely not. The most I ever drank was the night I got sick, even then I didn't black out. Plus, Grizz would have never let anyone touch me."

I looked back at the tests. Kim was still talking but it sounded like static in my ears. What was I going to do? I started college in less than three weeks. I couldn't have a baby. I had to tell my aunt, my parents, and Grizz.

I could finally hear Kim again. "...It says right here." She was reading off her phone, "Human and Shifter DNA is thought to be incompatible. There have been no successful matings between Human and Shifter since the race was first discovered. This shouldn't be able to happen."

I grabbed her by the arm and pulled her out of the bathroom, "Come on. You have to take me to Grizz. Right now."

We got to the compound twenty minutes later. The ride seemed to take forever. Shifters were required by law to live secluded from the towns they inhabited. Most lived in communal buildings like the compound. It was to give them room and privacy to shift when they wanted, since it was illegal to do in normal society. I would have given anything for it to be closer to town. I had to have Kim stop once for me to throw up again.

That time I thought it was nerves, not pregnancy.

We pulled up and Grizz's bike was right

outside. I sighed with relief. Getting out of the car,

I walked up to the door and went in, Kim right

behind me. Stepping inside, I scanned the room

for my baby's daddy. Oh, geez. The only person I

saw was Hutch, Grizz's younger brother and best

friend. He jumped to his feet.

"Zoey? What the fuck are you doing here?

Don't you usually come up on the weekend?" he

asked, walking toward me, cutting me off from

the stairs.

I moved around him. "I need to see Grizz.

There's something important I need to tell him."

He stepped in front of me again. "Now, Zoey, I think it would be best if you went on home. Maybe call Grizz, and let him know when you're coming."

I shoved past him and made for the stairs. Behind me, he growled in irritation.

"Don't say I didn't warn you!" he called.

I went down the hall, Kim only a step or two behind me, grabbed the doorknob, turned it and swept into the room. As I moved, I tried to think of what to say, how to tell him that I was going to have his baby. I wondered how he would react. Would he be excited? Scared? Upset? What I didn't expect was what I saw as we stepped through the door.

Grizz was on his back on the bed, the sheets and blankets tossed in a heap on the floor. He was naked, sweating, and thrusting up into a woman I didn't know. She sat straddling him, grinding her hips on him and massaging her own breasts. Grizz's hands gripped her hips as he pumped back and forth.

"Jesus fucking Christ! I fucking knew it, Zo!" Kim yelled, stepping around me.

Grizz and the girl stopped moving and turned to look at us. It would have been a little better, maybe, if they'd acted the least bit ashamed. If they'd at least pretended that what they were doing was wrong. But the girl didn't even try to cover herself up. She just looked at us in irritation.

Grizz frowned. "Hey, Zo, damn, were you coming over today?"

He didn't act disturbed at all that I had caught him fucking someone else. My chest heaved as I stared at him. I'd thought we were in love. It looked like that had only been a one-way street.

The skank flipped her hair over her shoulder. "Yo, ladies, um, I was trying to get some dick. Can you back the fuck out for like another ten minutes?" My skin crawled hearing her speak.

Grizz waved a hand at her and slid out from beneath the woman's sweaty legs. He grabbed his boxer shorts and slid them on, standing up with his dick still mostly hard.

Kim grabbed my arm. "Let's just get the hell out of here. You don't need this piece of shit."

I didn't know what to do. My vision blurred from tears, and all I could do was blurt out what I wanted to say. "I'm pregnant."

Grizz frowned at me. "Okay, so?"

"It's your baby, Rhett, we're having a baby." I wiped tears from my cheeks I hadn't even realized were there.

He laughed at me. He actually laughed at me. An icy pain blossomed in my chest, like he'd stabbed me directly in the heart.

"Zo, I don't know what game you're playing here. I mean, we've had a lot of fun. But if you're knocked up, you need to go find the daddy. Stop trying to trap me in some shit that is, bear with me now, physically...impossible."

Kim waved her finger at Grizz. "Hey! Fuck you, Grizz. The only person she's been with is you. You and your filthy little bear cock. Asshole!"

Grizz's face grew dark and he snarled at Kim. My friend didn't back down, and I loved her for it.

"Grizz? Rhett? You have to believe me," I whispered with my blood pounding in my ears. "It's your baby."

He looked at me a little softer. "I don't need all this, okay? If you can't keep track of who you've fucked, and who knocked you up then maybe just get rid of the thing!" Grizz's expression hardened again. "Now, get the hell out of here, and don't come back!"

My jaw dropped again. How could he be so cruel and heartless? This was the man I'd fallen in love with. He was so angry, without a hint of the kindness he'd shown me the last several weeks. Fresh tears fell as I tugged at Kim's sleeve and turned away from the first person I ever truly loved. At least, I thought I'd loved him.

Kim turned around on the way out and yelled back, "Have fun with that skinny dick, bitch!"

She slammed the door behind us. I stumbled down the hallway, numb. At the stairs I saw Hutch, his arms crossed, looking both ashamed and angry.

"I told ya, didn't I? I told ya! It's just —"

"Fuck off," Kim said, cutting him off.

Kim drove me back to Aunt Patty's house. She tried to talk to me along the way, bad-mouthing Grizz and Hutch. Tried to apologize for ever introducing me to them. All I could do was stare at the floorboard the whole ride home.

Aunt Patty knew something was wrong as soon as we walked in. I fell apart, sobbing, and told her everything. Grizz, the sex, the baby, everything. She never shamed me or scolded me either. She just let me cry and told me everything was going to be all right.

After I'd calmed down, Kim asked, "What are you going to do, Zo?"

My tears dried and I clenched my jaw. "I'm keeping the baby. I'll do it on my own, I don't need Grizz."

"Girl, you aren't alone. I'll do whatever I need to do to help you out," Kim said.

Patty hugged me again. "Well, Zo, one thing is for sure. As poorly as this trip has ended, you've found a true friend. And those are way more important than some man who doesn't want to take responsibility for what he's done." She met my gaze. "Are you ready to call your parents?"

I took a deep, steadying breath, and nodded.

The call was long and not as torturous. Lots more tears, but no shouting or angry words. Mom and Dad told me they would help me get through anything. We made plans for school, getting home, and all that would come after. They were here for me, they promised, and their love made my tears fall faster. I was right, I didn't need Rhett "Grizz" Allen in my life. I would raise this baby as my own, and if it was a boy, I would raise him to

be a better man than his father.

Chapter 1 - Grizz

The party raged around me. My guys were having the time of their lives. Girls kept coming up to me and pawing at me, but I waved them off or pushed them away. I was way past caring about women. I kept slapping my phone against my leg every few seconds, irritation building with each moment that passed.

I'd received the call about thirty minutes ago, just before the party jumped off, telling me my little brother had gotten his ass kicked. Something about a rival gang. I didn't know the whole story yet. But, by god, I was gonna find out about it. Some of the boys were bringing Reck

back to the compound now.

The door to the compound slammed open

and Hutch leaned in, scanning the crowd for me. I

locked eyes with him. He tilted his head back

toward the garage outside. Nodding, I stood and

started that way, snatching up a bottle of beer

and nearly ripping the top off as I went out the

door.

"He got his ass handed to him, bro," Hutch

said.

I took a drink from the bottle and looked

sideways at him, waiting for more.

"Probably four or five guys. Beat him down

pretty well. At least three broken ribs, a broken

finger, a broken nose, and maybe the orbital bone. Says his head hurts too. Might be a fractured skull. He's already healing, though. Won't outwardly see a scratch by tomorrow, but he'll be sore as shit for a day or two."

One of the many benefits to being born shifters was the accelerated healing. It took a *lot* to kill a shifter. Though I kind of wished Reck could feel the pain for more than a couple days. It might teach him a lesson.

I finished the bottle and chucked it as far as I could. It shattered against the side of an old truck sitting with flat tires behind the garage. I didn't say anything. Nothing really needed to be said. Hutch knew what I was thinking.

Fighting back my anger, I ripped the door open and walked through. Reck sat on a rolling stool with an ice pack on his face. Three of the guys hung around near him, waiting for me. I looked at them, then pointed at the door with my thumb.

I glared at Reck while the others, minus Hutch, made their way out. Reck sat with the ice pack on his face, staring at his shoes.

The door clicked shut and I asked, "Is there a reason this has become a regular occurrence? Can you explain why I am always dealing with some kind of shit you get into?"

Reck threw the ice pack to the ground. "Grizz, man! Don't you want to at least hear what happened?"

I stepped toward him, angry at his tone. "I don't need to know what happened. I already know you! But if you feel it will help me understand, please feel free."

Reck nodded and sucked in a shaky breath. "Okay. Was that so hard? Anyway, I was down at this bar just outside Boise. Like, forty minutes away. I was talking to a chick, and some dude decided he didn't like me talking to her. I guess they were a thing. I didn't even know who her old man was when we started talking. Turns out it was a guy who was a member of that gang we had an issue with two years ago. You know the ones?

So he gets mad and his dudes jump me. That's it."

I looked at him with my eyes narrowed. I

could almost smell the bullshit as I stared at him

for several seconds, not saying anything. Letting

the moment build.

"Talking? That's it?" I asked.

Reck leaned back in his chair and threw his

hands up in surrender. "Fine! All right? Fine. I was

getting my dick sucked in the bathroom."

I bit the inside of my cheek to keep from

screaming at him. Instead, I gritted my teeth and

held my temper. "And the guy?"

"Yeah...I maybe knew he was the head

honcho of that gang when I started putting the

moves on the girl. I didn't think we'd get caught there though. I took a picture of her doing it with my phone. I was going to send it to him later to just fuck with him. You know?"

In one quick step, I was on him. My hand cracked across the back of his head. "You are not a kid anymore! You have *got* to stop being such a reckless asshole! Do you understand me? I am the leader of this gang! I am the Alpha of this Clan. You will do as I say, do you understand?"

Reck fell forward, clutching his still sore skull in his hands. I hurt him pretty bad. He could only nod. I thought I saw his breath hitch as though he was crying.

My anger already fading, I sighed at my little brother. "Go sleep it off."

Reck nodded and got up, ignoring my stare as he shuffled out. But then he made a slight detour and grabbed a half-empty bottle of Jack Daniel's from a work table on his way. As soon as the door closed behind him, Hutch looked at me and laughed. "Jesus, it's like having a kid, right?"

I laughed too. It was true. Honestly, Reck was the closest I had to a kid. I'd basically raised the little shit once Mom and Dad died. I hadn't done such a good job, it looked like.

Hutch mentioning a kid brought a brief flash of memory to that summer nine years ago. A beautiful brown-haired girl. We'd fooled around all summer. Then, all of a sudden she'd gone crazy and tried to say I'd knocked her up. She hadn't seemed like the psycho clinger type at first, but looks were deceiving.

"Bro, you good?" Hutch asked.

I blinked. "What do you mean?"

"Well, you were kinda just staring off into space."

I shrugged. "Just trying to imagine all the ways I'm going to kill our baby brother if he can't get his shit together."

Hutch scrubbed his hands over his face. "You want to go back to the party? Find a piece of tail to get your mind off it?"

Even that didn't sound like fun. "Not in the mood. I'm going for a run," I said, walking out the door.

I started running and quickly shifted into my bear form. I'd always felt more alive like that. I could smell so much more, hear so much more. It's like I was really *living* in the world. Actually a part of it. I needed to clear my head and nothing beat shifting for that. I ran as fast as I could, deep into the forest, my breath chuffing out of my snout.

Jesus, it's almost like having a kid, right?

Hutch's words came back to me. I couldn't get them out of my mind. That girl, what was her name again? I felt bad that I couldn't remember it.

I'd taken her virginity and couldn't remember her name?

Whatever, it had been almost a decade, and there'd been a lot of girls since then. I remembered she had been sweet. I really did hope she'd found out who the daddy was. I hoped her life had turned out okay.

The next morning I got to the shop early. I liked to get in early and make sure everything was in order and ready for the day. While I waited for the overhead lights to warm up, I pulled up the day's schedule on the shop computer. It looked like a busy day, which is always good. Running a legitimate and profitable business was actually more difficult than running a gang. Or a pack.

As the day wore on, I settled into the rhythm. Even though I owned the place, I was usually out with the staff turning wrenches. I liked manual labor. It kept me grounded, or at least that's what I thought.

Several of the first few appointments we had were women, and as usual there wasn't really anything wrong with the cars. This was a daily occurrence. They came in and gave some vague description of an issue. Then while the guys tried to troubleshoot the problem, the ladies hovered around and flirted.

Everyone that worked for me was a shifter, it was very well known, and we all had the visible tattoo showing our mark. Fucking a shifter was apparently the height of eroticism, and women came from further away than Boise to try to get into my boys' pants. I was sure some of them succeeded. I didn't tell my guys what they could or couldn't do once they were off the clock. Plus, I still got to charge for the diagnostics and whatever else we did to the car. Win-win for me.

I had one more appointment before lunch, so I sent the others on break. I would do this last job myself. It was just scheduled to be an oil change and system check. Ticket said it'd be a black Camaro. About five minutes after my crew left for lunch, I spotted the car I was waiting for turn into the parking lot and slowly make its way through the garage doors.

With a sigh for the female silhouette I could just see behind the wheel, I turned around and pulled a handheld diagnostics reader from the toolbox and primed the oil pump. Ready to fend off a flirtatious woman, I heard the door open and close behind me.

Without turning around, I asked, "How are you today? It's a nice one, isn't it?"

A sharp intake of breath, almost like a gasp, drew my attention quickly. I turned around, an eyebrow raised in question, to find a gorgeous woman standing there, her hand on the car, almost holding herself up.

Why was she looking at me so weird? Then I started to see what I hadn't noticed before. That hair, the hazel eyes, those lips. I remembered. The memory of that summer slammed into me like a freight train.

Jesus Christ, *she* was here? After all these years, she was here? Now that she was in front of me, and I could see her, I remembered how much fun we'd had that summer.

She straightened up and her nostrils flared. "Are—are you the owner?"

I wiped my hands on my work pants. "I am."

She pursed her lips and shook out her hair. "Great, I need an oil change and a once-over of everything else."

"Uh...yeah, I know," I said dumbly. She'd been pretty then. She was glorious now.

"Okay, great. How long?" She acted like I was a complete stranger. I was confused. This *was* the girl. I knew it. Like a flash, I remembered her name! Zoey! But...I was pretty sure she preferred it shorter. Zo? That sounded right. "Do you not recognize me?"

She stared at me blankly, almost as if I hadn't said a word.

I pointed at my chest like a dumbass, and said, "Grizz? Rhett Allen? We spent a whole summer together?"

She frowned and squinted, like she was pretending her eyes were bad and she couldn't get a good look at me.

"I'm sorry, it doesn't ring a bell," she said.

Getting irritated, I finally blurted out, "I took your virginity? I mean, sorry, but that has to jog the ol' memory."

She shook her head and laughed without humor. "Sorry, big guy. You've got the wrong lady. I'll be back in an hour, is that enough time?"

I stared at her for a few seconds before I gave in. She wanted to play it dumb. Okay, then. "Sure, yeah. An hour."

She turned. "Thanks." I couldn't take my eyes off of the beauty as she walked out the door, across the street, and out of sight without bothering to look back. I just stood there, dumbstruck, watching her leave.

Once she was gone, I *still* stood there, so confused. How could she have forgotten me? I'd been her first, and hell, I sure as shit remembered mine. Had she lied back then?

Maybe she hadn't been the innocent little flower I'd thought she'd been. Either that, or I just wasn't very memorable.

I laughed out loud. Yeah, right. She'd had as much fun as I had until she tried to pin a pregnancy on me.

As I started working on her car, one question kept bouncing around my head. *What did you do with the kid?*

Chapter 2 - Zo

I kicked the booth in front of me. A heavy thump accompanied my motion under the table. It felt good, so I kicked it again, harder. The diner server glanced up, so I stopped.

I was so incredibly pissed at myself. I had, literally, spent years thinking about what I would say to Grizz if I ever ran into him. I'd even given myself a few pep talks and practiced in my head on the five-day drive up here. I'd done it because I knew it was entirely possible I would at least see him. Forest Heights was still as tiny as it had been nine years ago. Everybody knew everybody.

But, come on! The very first week? Really? I should have been able to get at least a couple more days in. Have some time to acclimate before seeing his face. My luck was apparently terrible. I just wanted to make sure my car had survived the thousand-mile journey she, Rainer, and I had made.

Rainer. The thought of him put a knot in my stomach. I glanced out the diner window at the open door to the garage across the street. When I'd laid eyes on Grizz again, it had been like looking at an older version of my boy. It made my heart hurt. I decided then that this would be the last time I would speak to Grizz. Once my car was done, we were done.

My phone started vibrating, and it was Rainer.

I answered, "Yes, babe?"

"Hey! Mom?"

"This is your mother, yes," I said sarcastically.

He chuckled. "Okay, yeah. Could you maybe stop and get ice cream on the way home?"

Distantly, sounding like she was across the room, I heard Kim call out, "Sundaes! I said get stuff for sundaes! Cherries, whipped cream, the whole nine yards!"

"Oh, yeah! Sundaes. Can you, Mom?" Rainer asked.

I laughed and said I would. Why the hell

not? I could use some sugar therapy at this point.

It had actually been Kim's idea anyway. Any time

she visited, she spoiled Rainer rotten.

When I'd told her I was moving to Forest

Heights to take care of Aunt Patty, she'd just

about jumped at the chance to move back home

too. She'd gone to California for college, and I'd

done a half-year at Texas before transferring back

home to the University of South Carolina after

Rainer was born.

Mom and Dad had helped me so much

through college. They'd been disappointed in me

for getting pregnant, but they had never stopped

loving me or Rain, up until the day they'd died in a car wreck.

My phone buzzed again. Thinking Rainer was calling back to see if I could maybe buy a cotton candy machine too, I picked it up. Instead it was a text.

Car's done.

How eloquent. I laid five dollars on the counter to pay for my coffee and a tip. I smiled at the server on the way out, and tried to mentally prepare myself for seeing Grizz again. Moving quickly, I hurried my steps to get there and give him as little time as possible to see me coming. Great idea that was, seeing as he was standing outside the garage door, already waiting for me.

He opened his mouth to say something, but I cut him off.

"Can I go ahead and see my bill?" I asked.

He was definitely irritated, but he put a fake grin on and nodded. He was only gone for a minute before he returned with a printout of the bill and my keys.

I took the paper and skimmed through it, making sure I wasn't overcharged.

This obviously made him even more agitated. "Oil change and diagnostics check. That's it. I did wash it on the house, though," he said in a clipped tone.

I didn't answer. Mostly because I didn't know what to say. Instead, I pulled my card out of my pocket and handed it over. He took it, but just stared at me for several seconds.

"You really don't remember me?" he asked.

I shrugged. "Hey, it was a pretty wild summer for me. A lot of stuff happened. I'm sure we must have had fun though."

The lie caused his perpetual scowl to deepen. He sighed and took the card back to the office and was back in two minutes with a receipt.

He handed them to me, along with my keys. "Thanks," I muttered.

Whirling, I walked to my car as fast as I could without it seeming like I was hurrying. I wouldn't give him the satisfaction.

He called out to me, "How long are you going to be in town?"

I almost let myself slide back in time, back to the night of the party. The night I met him, and he asked me almost the exact same question. Instead, I shook my head sadly. "Why do you care?"

He just looked at me, a little forlorn, a little exasperated, just as hard as he'd always been. "Just curious."

I didn't allow any external reaction as I slid into the car, but before closing the door, I called out to him, "I'll be here as long as I need to be." With a heavy heart, I drove away without looking back at him, so damn proud of myself that I wasn't crying.

When I got to the grocery store, I walked through several aisles in a daze. Sundaes. That was what I was supposed to be getting, but heck if I could remember what went on them.

Somehow, I found myself in the checkout lane, my cart filled with all the items needed for sundaes, as well as two frozen pizzas to complete the super nutritious dinner we would have tonight.

I got to Kim's house and sat in the driveway with my motor running. I couldn't sit as long as I wanted to because the ice cream was slowly melting in the trunk. Sighing deeply, I opened the door. Inside, I put the bags on the counter as Kim came in to help. Her smile froze when she saw my face.

Rainer ran into the kitchen and eagerly dug through the bags, looking for the ice cream and toppings.

Kim patted his shoulder. "Hey, bud, go wash your hands first, okay?"

"Oh, man! Fine," he said and went toward the guest bathroom.

Kim looked me dead in the eye and said, "You look like shit. What happened?"

"Jeez, you really know how to talk to a girl," I said.

"Give it up," Kim said.

"I took the car to the shop," I said.

"Okay. And?"

With my nostrils flaring, I kept my voice even. "Grizz owns the fucking shop. He was *there*. Like, he was literally the only person there when I got there. It was as awkward as you could imagine." I sighed. "And then some."

Kim slapped a hand on her forehead and moaned. "Oh, shit! Zo, I swear I didn't know. Really, I didn't. It's been years since I was back home. I mean, hell, the garage wasn't even *there* when I left. It was like a dry cleaner or something back then."

I shook my head and squeezed her arm. "No, it's not your fault. You couldn't have known."

I should've checked. I should've social media

stalked or searched the internet. Anything to know where he'd be so I could make sure and *not* be there.

As I helped her put away the groceries, I tried to deal with the shock of seeing Grizz so soon after coming back. Kim and I had discussed what we would do if I met up with him again. Would I ever try to tell him about Rainer again, mainly. If Grizz ever caught sight of my boy, he wouldn't be able to deny it. He looked so much like Grizz, it was crazy.

For nine years, I'd searched for stories, even a hint of a rumor, of a shifter getting a human pregnant. I'd never found anything in all that time. And every test I'd undergone before Rainer was born, and every test my son had? They all came back normal. My boy was human. The thing that caused me to wake up in cold sweats some nights was the thought that, maybe, the bear part of him was just lying dormant. Maybe when he hit puberty, or even ten years old, it would manifest.

Living in the same town, I knew I would eventually have to tell Grizz, but until that time was upon me, I didn't have to do anything. I would keep the secret as long as physically possible. If he never shifted, I'd never have to deal with that lying, cheating, no-good bear again.

"*Ice cream*!" Rainer yelled as he ran back into the kitchen.

I laughed, pushing all thoughts of Grizz Allen out of my mind. My son was my sole focus. Always had been, always would be. The bear was irrelevant at the moment. Only my son and his happiness mattered.

Chapter 3 - Grizz

It had been a few days since I'd seen Zoey. Her name had been on the credit card, and it had all come back to me when I saw it. *Zoey-goes-by-Zo.* It felt like yesterday. I couldn't get her out of my head, though.

I frowned and winced. The music from the party seemed louder than usual. It was smaller than the last, but seemed more manic, more annoying. Part of my foul mood was the fact that my pride was a little wounded. It really had seemed like she didn't remember me. That kind of thing really took a lot out of you. It had seemed to me, at the time, that we'd had a pretty good thing going that summer. Maybe I'd been wrong. I could even remember the day she'd walked in on me with that other girl.

She'd just been another shifter groupie. A quick lay. I hadn't thought anything about it at the time. Zoey and I weren't official. It had been a summer fling, no strings.

Yet, I could still see her look of horror even now, though. Whatever she'd been about to lie to me about the baby, it had really hurt her to see me in bed with... whoever it had been.

But hell, I'd been a dumbass kid back then. It wasn't any wonder Reck was such a wild little shit now, if I was what he had to look up to.

A soft hand touched my shoulder and slid around to my chest. I turned to find Candy, one of my go-to girls, usually. She smiled and bit her lower lip, letting her hand slide across my stomach toward my jeans.

But I was not in the mood. I pushed her hand away and said, "Go find another dick to suck. I've got stuff on my mind."

She pulled back and looked at me with a pissed-off expression. "Hey, fuck you, Grizz!"

"Not tonight you won't," I said without looking at her.

"Asshole!" She stomped away.

Five minutes later, Hutch sidled up to me. "Bro, what the fuck did you do to piss off Candy?

She's out back crying with a couple of chicks, talking shit about you. I think you hurt her feelings."

I sighed. "Do you remember, back in the day, that chick that tried to make us think I'd gotten her knocked up?"

Hutch frowned and furrowed his brows. "Yeah. How could I forget that? She caught you balls deep in another girl too, if I remember right."

I rubbed a hand roughly across my face, feeling ashamed of that part again. "Well, that same girl came by the shop today to get her car serviced."

Hutch's jaw dropped. "For real? Jesus, it's been like ten years! What did she want?"

"Nine years," I corrected. "She just wanted the service. Acted like she didn't even recognize me! I fixed her car up, she came back, and I asked again if she remembered me. She said she had a real crazy summer that year. Apparently, I didn't even rate."

Hutch laughed and slapped me on the back. "That's what you get for being a cocky sonofabitch all the time."

I turned and snarled at him, then growled low in my throat. I wasn't actually angry at him, but I needed an outlet.

To my irritation, Hutch kept chuckling. "Yeah, yeah, big bad bear. Anyway, you gonna try to get a hold of her? Seem to remember she was a hot little thing."

"She doesn't mean anything to me, Hutch. She's just a chick I hooked up with," I said. She'd been cool, though. I'd been bummed about her coming up with that bullshit story about the baby. We could've hung out a lot longer.

"Well, I think you meant something to her. Dude, she looked like run-over dog shit the day she left after catching you with that chick. That much I do remember. You don't fake that." Hutch whistled and shook his head sadly.

I looked at him, unable to deny the truth to myself. I could lie to him all day. "She was sad because she wanted to trap me with a baby. Some other dude's baby at that."

Hutch shrugged. "I don't know. Seemed like more than that at the time."

My brother didn't say more, and I didn't press him. I just wanted Zo out of my head. It made me feel strange inside when I thought about her. It made me feel...dirty somehow.

"I mean...do you think she ever really was pregnant?" Hutch asked, pulling me out of my thoughts.

I shrugged. How did I know? "Maybe. She disappeared before she could ever start showing. I didn't see a kid with her today at the shop, and no sign in the car, but maybe."

Hutch looked at me weird. "If she was? Do you think the kid could have been yours?"

He'd lost his damn mind. "You and I both know that it's not possible. Zero percent chance."

But my mind kept going back to that first night with Zo. She'd been a virgin, I knew that for sure, and she'd spent so much time with me that summer. When would she have had time to knock boots with some other asshole? The idea, impossible as it was, wouldn't get out of my head now that Hutch had voiced it.

"Right, yeah. But, let's talk to Dax. If there's anyone who would know for sure, he would."

Dax was the eldest member of the pack and the gang. He'd run the woods with my old man, way back in the day. No one knew how old he was for sure. I figured he had to be almost sixty, but he looked really good for his age.

I nodded wearily and followed Hutch inside. We moved between people and tables. One of the gang had his back against the wall, a girl on her knees in front of him.

"Hey, go to a fucking room!" I yelled. "That's why we have them!"

He pulled his pants up and dragged the girl to the stairs, his face red with embarrassment. I hated to admit it, but yelling at someone made me feel a little better. Especially since I was going along on this pointless mission with my brother.

We found Dax coming out of one of the back rooms, zipping his pants with a grin. A girl who couldn't have been older than twenty, emerged from behind him. Her hair was a mess, and she pulled her skirt up as she walked past us. I looked at Dax and shook my head with a smile.

"Dude, she's young enough to be your granddaughter," Hutch said.

Dax stretched. "There's no judgment with the lights off. She didn't seem to mind an old bear's body."

I clapped the dirty old man on the back. "We need to talk to you about something. You got a minute?"

"Sure," he said. "I need about thirty minutes before my trusty rifle is ready for round two." He patted his crotch when he said it.

We went back to the heart of the party and grabbed a few drinks at the bar. I led Dax and Hutch to the table furthest away from anyone. I didn't want someone to overhear what we were going to talk about.

Dax took a drink and then eyed us. "All right, boys. The hell ya want?"

I looked at Hutch, who raised his eyebrows and shrugged. No help there. "Dax, in all your time, have you heard of any bear...well, hell, any shifter really, having a kid with a human?"

Dax sat up rigid, and his hand nearly crushed the glass in his hand. I almost sat back, he looked so ready to slug me.

Through gritted teeth, Dax said, "Why do you need to know?"

The reaction was *not* what I expected. It was so far removed from Dax's normal personality, it almost made me nervous. The tendons stood out on his neck.

I tried to get the story out as best as I could. "I had a little fling with a girl about nine years ago. Toward the end of summer, she came to me and said she was pregnant. Said it was my baby. I basically told her to, well, I wasn't a great person about it. I told her to get lost and not come back.

She's back in town now, and Hutch and I just wanted to know if there was even a, like, half a percent chance it could have happened."

Dax relaxed slowly as I spoke. When I was done, he lifted his glass and drained the rest of his drink before slamming the glass down and wiping his lips with the back of his hand.

"Fuck," Dax said.

Hutch and I locked eyes, neither one of us knowing what the hell was going on.

Almost too low to hear, Dax whispered, "I guess it's time to tell you," He looked at us then and continued. "I'm about to tell you boys something that only your daddy knew. And he took the secret to the grave with him. Can I trust you?"

Hutch and I both nodded. I was too intrigued to bring up the fact that I was the Alpha and should've been above reproach.

Dax took a deep breath and looked around before continuing in a quiet voice. "My daughter has a human mother."

I sat back so fast my chair rocked on its feet. I would have been less surprised if Dax had told me he was secretly a vampire. A human mother? How?

Dax went on, "Same sorta story you had. Had a few wild nights with a tight little thing. After a few months, I could tell she was pregnant. I thought like you did. Must have been banging some other dude, or maybe a couple of dudes. I sent her on her merry way. A few years later, she turns back up. I saw the kid, and by god, I could see it right there. She looked just like me when I was little. We had a DNA test done, it came back one hundred percent. I was the daddy."

I could see Dax's daughter in my mind. Everyone knew her, she was around my age. I could actually remember us playing together when I was eight or nine years old. I didn't think anyone had ever seen her mom though.

"So, I took the little girl in. raised her up just like I hadn't missed a day. I was worried. Right? I mean, damn, what would the government do if they found out we could get humans knocked up? Her mother agreed. We were both afraid the damn Men in Black or something would show up and take our baby away. Fuckin' vivisect her or torture her with experiments, god only knows what. And I will tell you this, Grizz, there have to be more of them out there. I'm not special. There is a chance you are that kid's daddy. If you go by the math I have to work with, it's a lot better than a one percent chance."

Hutch looked as stunned as I felt as he lowered his head into his hands. Probably contemplating how many humans he'd had sex with without protection, if I had to guess. A cold sweat broke out across my body. Fucking shit. I had to get out of here. I had to clear my head. I feel like I might have a panic attack, a strange feeling for me. I always kept control, a level head.

I pushed back from the table and stood. "Thanks, Dax. I just need a minute."

"Helluva kick in nuts, ain't it, boy?" Dax asked, leaning across the table to pick up the rest of my drink and finish it himself.

I walked as quickly as I could to the back door, then pushed out into the night air. As fast as I could, I took in a couple of deep breaths, and still didn't feel any better. Usually, I didn't take my clothes off to shift, but I felt constricted, tight as a drum. I wanted to run as free as I could. I pulled everything off and left it in a pile outside the door before sprinting to the edge of the woods, my body changing as I went.

In bear form, everything seemed a little less oppressive. I could actually think without freaking out. All this time, and shifters could mate with humans. I knew why Dad hadn't told me. It wasn't his secret to tell; it was Dax's. But, damn! This was shit every shifter should know was a possibility. To just get hit with this news out of nowhere was not cool.

My bear form couldn't drown out the other emotions coursing through me. Guilt. Raging unquenchable guilt. If Zo had told me the truth all those years ago? I'd broken her goddamn heart. I hurt a sweet girl who hadn't done anything wrong

other than get involved with an asshole like me.
And I'd lost eight years with a child that might've
been mine.

I thought about all the memories I had of
Mom and Dad when I was six, seven, eight. I'd
missed over eight years of my child's life. *If,* I
reminded myself, *if* the kid was mine. None of it
sat well with me. As I crashed through the woods,
I made plans to find Zo tomorrow. Find her, and
find out the truth.

Chapter 4 - Zo

I was in Aunt Patty's kitchen, prepping meals for her. The stroke, thankfully, hadn't been severe enough to damage her brain. That part of her was fine. It was the fall she'd taken at the time of the stroke that had done the most damage. She'd broken her hip, and now had to move around the house in an electric wheelchair for several more months before moving to a walker, and then, hopefully, back to walking on her own. Being a nurse already, I had been more than happy to move here and help out. Both Idaho and South Carolina allowed nurses to work across state lines without needing an additional license, so Aunt Patty's insurance was actually paying me to be here, too. It worked out great all around. It just made me feel so bad watching her putter around the house in that tiny little chair.

One of the few things she really wasn't able to do was cook. So I'd told her I would prep a bunch of meals each week that she could pop out easily and heat up. It would let her have a little independence, being able to get her own food ready.

I could hear Rainer upstairs, his tablet volume was way too loud, but I didn't have the energy to yell at him to turn it down. I'd promised to take him to the park later, too. I had to do that pretty often. He had so much energy. He was super active, and had a monster metabolism. I was going to go broke feeding him when he became a teenager. It must have been the bear in him.

The buzz of the wheelchair entering the room warned me to put a happy expression on my face as Aunty Patty came in.

"How's it feel doing all those years of nursing school to end up a line cook?" Patty asked.

I laughed and closed the lid on a pasta salad I had just finished. "Well, it beats changing bedpans for handsy old men in a hospital."

Patty chuckled. "Seriously, how do you feel to be back?"

I thought for a moment and took a deep breath as I decided to be honest. "I'm worried, I guess. I have this bad feeling something is going to go wrong."

Patty reached up and squeezed my arm. "Listen, you have to understand that Grizz might find out about Rainer. You're going to be here a while. The odds of him seeing our boy are pretty high. It's just something that might happen. And none of this is your fault. You tried telling the son of a bitch back when it all first happened."

I hated this. If only we could stay hidden. But keeping Rainer inside forever wasn't remotely a possibility. "Yeah, I know. I just worry that if Grizz finds out, he may try to take Rainer from me. I won't allow that!"

Before Patty could respond, a knock at the door drew our attention. Patty backed her chair up to give me room. I slid the pasta salad into the fridge and walked out of the kitchen and through the living room to the front door. Who would be here in the middle of the day? It was still an hour before the night nurse was supposed to show up. I glanced behind the curtains and my heart turned to ice.

Grizz was outside, looking around Patty's front porch with his hands in his pockets.

"Oh, shit," I whispered to myself.

Grizz cocked his head but didn't look. Had he heard me? Maybe not. He stood for a few more minutes before knocking again.

Even though I saw his hand and knew he was about to knock, I flinched at the sound. I debated just pretending that we weren't home, but that wouldn't work. Rainer would hear the knocking soon and come investigate. I couldn't let that happen. And Grizz could probably tell somehow that there were people inside.

Nothing for it. I opened the door just big enough for my head and leaned out.

"Can I help you? Why are you here?" I asked.

"I need to talk to you about something." He looked at his shoes, glanced at me, then back at his shoes.

"Is it about my car? Something you didn't tell me at the shop?" Go away!

Grizz sighed and looked at the sky before glancing back at me. "I know you remember me, Zo. You don't just up and forget the guy who got you pregnant."

I stiffened and stepped further out the door, blocking the rest of interior the house from his view with my body.

He could see the look on my face, though, and he raised his hands in surrender. "Hey, I just want to talk okay?"

I couldn't let him catch sight of Rainer. I stepped out onto the front steps, letting the door close to just a crack. I hadn't noticed it yesterday at the shop, I'd been in too much shock, but he'd gotten taller and broader. Grizz was now a mountain of a man, even more imposing than he had been all those years ago. Had he been so young then, too? It had seemed like he was older and wiser. Definitely more experienced. But he'd just been a kid too, really. Except even as a kid, he'd been far worldlier than me.

"What do you want?" I asked.

"I just...oh, hell...I just wanted to know the truth. About before? The baby you said was mine?" Grizz asked.

I stared at him a moment, fighting my heaving chest. "Okay, Rhett, Grizz, whatever you go by now. You don't have anything to worry about. There never was a baby. I made a mistake."

"What? Are you serious?" he asked, confused.

He narrowed his eyes at me like I was lying, and even though I was, it still pissed me off.

"Look, I don't have any reason to lie! My period was super late, I got freaked out and thought I was pregnant. False alarm, and a freaked out eighteen-year-old girl. That's all, okay?"

He looked at me hard for several moments before leaning back and sighing with relief.

Probably relief. The fact that he looked so grateful, that he didn't have to be a dad, let me know that I made the right choice in keeping Rainer a secret.

"Is that all you needed?" I asked.

He nodded, already stepping down from the porch. "It was, yeah."

I did have one question. "Why did you all of a sudden decide I might have been telling the truth? It would have meant a lot more back then, you know," I said. "A *lot* more."

He shrugged and frowned. He was fighting something internally, trying to figure out the right thing to say. "I guess I was just curious. I saw you yesterday, and I wanted to know for sure."

"Well," I said. "Your curiosity can now be satisfied."

He looked me up and down, not in a lewd way, more like he was really seeing me for the first time again. A smile broke out on his face. "You look really good."

"Thanks. You look old." I nodded at the gray strands in his beard.

He rubbed them and laughed before staring at me again, locking me in place with his eyes. It was the same as back then. When Grizz Allen looked at me, I knew that his attention was on me and only me. It was so intense. It used to melt me like nothing else. Now? That kind of intensity scared me.

Finally, he took his eyes off of me, and relief spread through me, like a weight being lifted off of my shoulders.

"Well, I appreciate you taking the time to talk. I really do," Grizz said. "Takes a load off."

A load off? What a jerk. I only nodded and held my breath as he walked to his truck, sighing in relief as he opened the door. He was almost gone. All I had to do was avoid him out and about in town, and we'd be good. Hope blossomed in my chest.

It was at that moment Aunt Patty's front door flew open behind me and Rainer came flying out the door running towards me. "Mom! Hey, there's a new game I need. Can we get it the next time we go to the store? It's awesome, I promise!" Rainer's words poured out of him rapidly.

Someone was squeezing my heart in their hand. *Oh, no.* Looking up, I caught sight of Grizz, his eyes locked on the boy, his mouth slowly falling agape. I was going to faint. The whole world was tilting sideways. Ignoring the ringing in my ears, I turned to put my body between Grizz and Rainer so he couldn't see him. "Baby, I will look at the game later. Just go back inside. Right now!"

He rolled his eyes at me and said sadly, "Yes ma'am."

My little guy's shoulders slumped as he turned to go. I whirled to find Grizz still staring at Rainer as he walked away. Grizz's gaze was locked, absolutely glued on *my* son.

I tried to mentally will Rainer to walk faster, but he stopped almost at the door and raised his head to sniff the air. No, no, not now. He turned around and sniffed again, this time looking at Grizz. My heart dropped.

Grizz looked like he was going to hyperventilate, his chest heaving up and down, a look of shock and...was that happiness? Or was it wishful thinking on my part?

I was about to open my mouth to again tell Rainer to go inside. But he cut me off.

Looking at Grizz, he cocked his head. "You smell like me?" Awe and confusion filled his voice.

I closed my eyes, trying my best to keep tears from streaming down my cheeks. Sucking in a few deep breaths to attempt to slow my stampeding heart, I prayed this wasn't really happening. When I opened them, Grizz had made his way from his truck and kneeled in front of my son.

He looked Rainer in the eye, but then turned and looked at me when he spoke. "There's a reason for that, little guy. There is a really good reason."

I finally snapped. "Damn it, Rainer! I said inside!"

Rainer whirled in shock. I never cussed at him. "But…" He stopped himself, seeing my face, then hung his head and walked to the porch. Remembering his manners, he mumbled, "Yes, ma'am," as he went up the steps.

Just before disappearing inside, he turned and waved to Grizz, who waved back. The door closed, and Grizz's expression changed from happy and awestruck to glaring at me. No way to get out of the conversation now.

Chapter 5 - Grizz

I was shaking, honest to God, shaking. It was like my entire body trembled like I was taking a jolt from a live wire. The boy! The boy looked just like me. There was no question in my mind. It was impossible to pinpoint how I was feeling right then. Pissed off at Zoey for lying to me, ashamed of myself for not believing her all those years ago, and sad, so fucking sad. All those years? Gone, and never coming back. I missed everything.

Of all those feelings, there was only one that I really knew, one that had been an old friend. Anger. I couldn't process any other thoughts right then. I knew how to be angry. So I turned it on Zoey.

"You lied to me," I spat.

Her face and chest went red. Not in fear though, I smelled zero fear. She was just as pissed off as I was. I didn't want to tell her, or admit to myself, she had every right to be.

She pointed her finger at me. "I don't know if you remember or not, but I *tried* to tell you. Almost ten years ago! If I remember correctly, you basically called me a whore who couldn't keep her legs shut and kicked me out of your life *while* another woman was literally on your dick! Given our final conversation, you can't really blame me for wanting to keep my boy a secret."

"*Our* boy," I corrected her.

"Don't you do that! Don't you fucking do that! Rainer is *my* son. I birthed him. Alone. I raised him. Alone. Taught him to be good and kind. Alone. He doesn't know you. And that, Rhett Allen, is your damn fault. Not mine."

My anger bubbled under the surface, though it was starting to turn away from Zoey and had begun to gnaw at me. I was angry with myself more than anything. But still, I kept it turned on Zoey. I didn't know another way to process it. "You could have come back at any time. After he was born. A year later, even two," I said.

Zoey laughed humorlessly. "Oh, sure."

It made me angry all over again, being laughed at like that. I let my teeth crush into my inner cheek, trying to keep myself in check.

She snarled her lip. "I have no doubt that the result would have been the same. I didn't feel like doing that to myself over and over again."

I stared at her, and knew that she was right. I would have never believed her. Not without seeing the kid the way he was now, and only after hearing that this was even possible at all.

With a long-suffering sigh, I tried to calm my voice before I spoke again. "Look, Zoey, I can't walk away from this. I can't. I mean..." I waved a hand at the house. "He looks just like me, so much like me, it's like I'm looking in a mirror to the past.

It blows my mind. I want to be part of his life."

How could I not? I wanted to break down just

thinking about all the time lost.

Zoey shook her head and held up her hand.

"That's going to take time, Grizz. A lot of time."

"I'm not patient by nature, okay? I want to

see my son," I said, trying to warn her. She had to

give a little.

She didn't sound angry anymore, just tired

when she said, "After eight years of raising Rainer

myself, I get to call *all* the shots. I'm in charge of

who does and doesn't see him. You don't have

any right to demand *anything*. Do you understand

that? You don't get to, because I gave you the

chance to be a dad all those years ago. And do you

know what you did? You showed me the door, called me a slut, and told me to never come back while your dick was wet with another girl's... Ugh. You know."

She was crying by the time she finished. I could finally see what I hadn't seen back then. I'd thought it was a summer fling. But Zoey had fallen for me.

I never noticed. And I'd ripped her fucking heart out. What a piece of work I was.

"Look," I said. "You have to see things from my perspective. There has never been a shifter and human baby. Never." Well, except one I couldn't mention. "You can't blame me for not believing, not entirely. It's like saying a dog and a cat had a baby."

Zoey nodded while wiping tears away. "No, Grizz, I get that. I really do. I spent an entire summer basically worshiping the ground you walk on. Then I found out the hard way that you really didn't give a damn about me. So I find out the first love of my life couldn't give two shits about me, *and* I found out I was eighteen and pregnant. That kind of sucks, right?"

My eyes were on the ground, rooted in place by the ten-fucking-tons of shame holding them in place.

Zoey went on. "I thought I meant something to you. If you'd really thought about it, you would have known you were the only person I'd been with that summer." She threw up her hands. "You would've at least talked to me. Told that other bitch to get out and had a real conversation."

A slide show flashed across my mind then. That summer, relived in a few quick memories. Our first night together, her virginity. I saw the way she'd looked at me, almost like worship. I didn't want to think about it, but she was right. Guilt, guilt, guilt. A truckload of it was starting to fill me up. I was consumed by it.

Zoey looked back at the house. "I need to talk to Rainer. I have to tell him who you are.

Because as far as he knows, he doesn't have a

father."

She couldn't have hurt me more. It felt like I

took an ice pick to the chest when she said that.

My boy grew up without a dad. He grew up

believing that he didn't even *have* a dad, all

because I'd been a selfish little prick.

I really didn't have any skin in this game. I

gave that up back then. Why the hell did I even

want to fight with her right now? Was it her fault I

was such an asshole back then? Bouncing from girl

to girl. What kind of father would I have been

back then, anyway? Probably shitty.

I decided to do the one thing I *never* did. I

backed down.

"Okay. Okay, Zo, I get it. You need the time to explain everything. That makes sense, take all the time you need." I backed up a few steps.

She looked at me like I was crazy for a second, then a hesitant smile slid into view.

"Just remember though, this changes everything. My life, your lives, they're all different now." He was my son. And I'd never be the same again. I wasn't sure I wanted to be.

I didn't wait for an answer. She knew all the places to find me. I turned and got into my truck as fast as I could and pulled away calmly, making sure not to screech the tires.

The drive back to the compound was filled with all the racing thoughts I had. My heart thudded in my chest, top speed. It was incredible to know that I had a boy out there. A beautiful boy. The part that broke my heart still was the fact that I missed so much. I kept coming back to that, circling around to the lost years. So much life, so many stories, so much I could have taught him, and so much he might have taught me.

Jesus, he'd be getting close to nine years old now. If he was a shifter, it could start soon. In a couple months maybe. Everyone shifted at a different time, but it was almost always between eight and ten. I'd never heard of anyone going later than twelve. Dear God, did he even know what was about to happen to him? His senses were far keener than a human. He'd been able to scent me and recognize the scent as something other.

My eyes tried to well up, but I shook my head hard, willing the tears to stay inside. I growled in rage as I turned up the gravel driveway to the compound, full of rage and sadness, each one warring with the other. It made me feel anxious in a way I'd never experienced before. I needed some type of release.

I skidded the truck to a halt in front of the compound and leaped out, my hands clenching and unclenching automatically at my sides. I took a massive, deep breath, scenting the air and smelling something in the distance. Deer? It was all I needed. It was close enough to run.

Taking off, I sprinted into the woods, shifting as I went. My skin vanished beneath fur, my teeth elongated into fangs, and my fingers twisted and warped into claws. It felt good to be a bear right then, so much less to think about. It was just me and a deer. A deer that had no idea what was coming for it.

Three hours later, I heard Hutch moving through the undergrowth toward me. I knew it was him long before he arrived. No one else smelled like Hutch, damn sawdust, beer, and motor oil. I was in my human form again, my stomach still achingly full. The carcass of the deer lay to my right on the edge of a small river that ran through the back of our property. I was scrubbing my hands in the water, trying to get the

blood out from under my nails. I already knew

what he was going to ask me about, and I didn't

know how to tell him without breaking down.

"What's up, bro?" Hutch asked, taking a

seat beside me.

I shook my head and kept my eyes on my

hands, scrubbing under the water.

"You good? How did it go?" Hutch sounded

worried. He knew.

I stopped moving my hands and took a deep

breath, then looked at him.

"I have a son." My throat sounded like I'd

been gargling with sandpaper or gravel.

Hutch looked like I'd just kicked him in the stomach.

He looked at the river, confusion all over his face. He said, "Are you sure?"

I laughed, "Hutch, if you saw this kid, you'd think someone built a time machine, and I ran out of it. There's zero question."

Hutch's face changed from shock to sadness. He picked up a rock and threw it into the river. But he had a big grin on his face. "Man, I've got a nephew! And, fuck, he doesn't even know me? I don't know him?"

I nodded. "I've been thinking the same thing for a few hours now."

Hutch wiped at his eyes with the back of his hand, to my surprise. Hutch was my brother, yes, but also the best friend I had. I knew him better than he knew himself, and he was not someone who got emotional. I let him compose himself.

Hutch finally sniffled and spoke. "What are we gonna do?"

I shrugged. "We have to wait. I don't get to dictate shit. I threw that out the window nine years ago. Zoey is his mom. Rainer's mom. That's his name, by the way!"

Hutch smiled at this, approving.

"She's the one who's taken care of him for damn near a decade. She knows what's best for him. I can only hope and trust that she'll do the

right thing and let me be a part of his life."

Chapter 6 - Zo

How was I supposed to tell my son all this mess? When he was little, around four, and he'd asked me where his daddy was, I couldn't exactly tell him that his father hadn't wanted him. I'd put him off as long as I could, eventually saying his daddy hadn't been ready to be a daddy yet. He'd accepted that, miraculously, and left me alone about it.

I'd expected Rainer to pounce as soon as I went back inside after talking to Grizz, but he hadn't. Another miracle.

For two days, all I'd done was worry about what and how I was going to tell my son that his father was back. Not back, he'd never been here to begin with. Here. Ugh.

It was all Kim and I had talked about. It was all Aunt Patty and I had talked about. And I was no closer to the perfect words than I had been the other day when I'd walked inside expecting an interrogation. But Rainer had run upstairs to play his video games.

Whoa. I was off the hook, for a short time, anyway.

"Mom?" Rainer asked as I rinsed off the breakfast dishes.

"Yeah?" I kept my voice guarded, not sure where he was going. Anything could come out of that kid's mouth. "What's up, buddy?"

"Would you care if I went to the daycare with Kim today?" he asked. "She said she gets some kids around my age in the summer."

He was getting bored with us. I'd figured this would happen. "Sure," I said. "Let me check with Kim and get Aunty Patty settled. Then I'll take you over there. You go get ready."

It was only a formality to check with Kim. She'd been so close all throughout Rainer's life. She was his godmother, and my best friend. We even had a pact to grow old together if we ended up single and over fifty. Me, Kim, and a house full of cats.

It was a plan. I pulled out my phone and texted my friend.

Can Rainer come hang with you today?

It took her a little while to reply. She liked to keep her phone in her office and not be on it when she was on the daycare floor, giving breaks or helping in the classrooms. When she did, I chuckled. It was just as I'd suspected.

Why do you even have to ask? Get my baby over here!

I smiled at my phone as I replied. Kim had been a constant presence. I'd do anything for the crazy woman. **He's not a baby anymore, Kimmy.**

Stop it. I don't want to hear that.

Still chuckling, I put my phone in my pocket. "Aunt Patty?" I called and went in search of the independent woman. I found her in the living room, all settled into the recliner. "You're not supposed to move out of the chair without me," I chided.

She waved me off. "I do what I want."

I sighed and made sure she had the remote, her drink, and her phone nearby. "I'm going to run Rainer over to the daycare. I'll be right back."

Patty waved. "Go. I'm fine."

"Rainer!" I called up the stairs. "Let's go!"

He bounded down and hugged his great-aunt, then we were off. It was nice to see he was in a good mood, hopeful about making friends. He hadn't exactly been happy about our move to Forest Heights, but he was a pretty laidback kid. He'd rolled with the punches.

The daycare wasn't a five-minute drive, but as soon as we backed out of the driveway, Rainer dropped the bomb. "Mom? Who was that man the other day?"

Aw, hell. "Who, now?" I knew darn well who he meant, but I still had no idea how to answer him.

"The man who smelled like me." He stared at me patiently from the passenger seat, totally buying that I was having a hard time remembering. Rainer was a big kid, just like Grizz had to have been. He was more than big enough to ride in the front seat, even at nine. But I was overly cautious and only let him when we were driving around town, probably not breaking thirty miles per hour. When we'd driven across the country, I'd made him ride in the back.

I realized he was still waiting on an answer while I thought about how big he was compared to his father. "What do you mean he smelled like you? Did he smell different from me?" I glanced at him as I turned on my turn signal.

Rainer shrugged. "Everyone has a different scent. You smell like me, too. I always figured it was because you're my mom." His senses had started to advance. I couldn't deny it now. He was going to shift into a bear. But when? "Aunt Patty smells similar," he continued. "Almost like everyone is a different flower. Similar, but different scents. But that man smelled just like me. Is..." He looked down at his hands. "Is he my dad?"

Aw, fuck, fuck, fuck! I hadn't wanted him to figure it out on his own. I'd totally failed my sweet boy.

"Oh, honey," I said and pulled into a gas station parking lot. "Have you noticed anything else? Besides being able to smell people?" As he shook his head, I totally avoided saying Grizz was Rainer's father. Way to go. But on the way for Rainer to spend the day at a daycare with my best friend wasn't the right time to admit that he had a

bear shifter for a father.

Of course, he knew shifters existed.

Everyone did. But how to tell someone they *were*

one? Especially a kid.

"So, who is he?" Rainer asked.

"That man's name is Rhett Allen. He goes by

Grizz. And he's the man who helped me make

you." Oh, way to cop out. I was such a coward

when it came to Rain.

He stared at the dash for a few seconds

before looking up at me with big, puppy dog eyes.

"So, he's ready to be a father now?"

Knife straight to my heart. He remembered

me saying that when he was so little. That poor

buddy. I wished he'd said something to me before now.

"Rain, buddy, I'm not sure. He says he is, but I don't want you hurt. We're going to take things really slow, okay?" I put my hand on his shoulder, wishing he would reach over for a big hug like he would've even a year ago.

But he nodded and faced forward again. "Okay, Mom. I think that's a good idea. Take things slow." He blinked several times. "I'm ready to go hang with Kim now."

He was pretty quiet until we pulled into the daycare center parking lot. "Mom?" Rainer asked. "Would you be upset if I wanted to have a dad?"

I put it in park but didn't turn off the air. It was too hot and muggy for that. "Gosh, no, buddy! Of course I expect you to want a dad. Anyone would. And I want you to have one, okay?"

He nodded and grinned eagerly. "We can give him a chance, right?" And to my intense pleasure, he leaned over and put his arms around my waist.

"Oh, my main man, of course we can. But the thing is, no matter what happens with Rhett, you've always, *always* got me, okay?"

He nodded against my shoulder. "Okay, Mom. Love you." He kissed me on the cheek just as Kim opened the front door and waved at us.

I watched my son bound inside, looking like a little kid again, eager to find other children his age to play with. Kim waved me off, unable to actually leave the building, so I headed back for Aunt Patty's.

"What's wrong?" she asked the minute she saw my face. "Something happened."

I threw my purse down and flopped onto Patty's sofa. "He asked me about Grizz."

She sighed and turned off the TV. "Well, we knew it was coming. What did you say?"

Rolling over, I stretched out and threw my arm over my face. "I told him the truth, gently. He wants to get to know Grizz, though he agreed to take things slow."

"Yeesh," Patty said. "Well, you know what you have to do now."

I did. "Oh!" I remembered the other part. Sitting up, I stared at my aunt. "Rainer is showing signs of being a shifter."

"I know," she said softly. "I was going to tell you soon. He sensed you coming in the house before he could've possibly known the other day. He either heard you or sensed you."

I slumped back down. "He's smelling people, too."

She chuckled. "That sounds unpleasant."

We shared a little laugh. "What do I have to do?" I asked.

"Sit down and talk to Grizz. It's obvious to us now that Rain is going to shift eventually. He's going to have to have that pack up there, as unsavory as they can be sometimes."

That was an understatement. "I won't let him around that rough crowd."

"No," Patty said. "Of course not. But they can come here. Rhett for sure. Maybe his brothers."

"Yeah," I said, my voice muffled by my arm. "But I don't wanna." I just wanted to cry.

She must've read my mood, though it was probably easy to do. "Cry," she said. "Rage. Get it all out now, here with me. Then you can keep your calm with Rhett and Rainer."

I screwed up my eyes to do as she'd said, but nothing happened. I just sighed. "I'll be okay. I always knew this day could come. Even if Rhett had denied it."

Once I helped Patty to the bathroom, I fixed lunch. While the grilled cheeses cooked, I texted Kim. **Could you keep R tonight? I'm going to go talk to Grizz.**

Kim must've been in her office for lunch, because she replied immediately this time. **Of course! We'll go see that new panda movie.**

I thanked her, then stared at my phone. Should I call him now or just show up at the shop?

Like a total chicken, I opted for showing up at the shop. When the night nurse came and relieved me at Patty's, I kissed her cheek and took off.

I didn't see him when I first got there, but Hutch sauntered out of the bay with a surprised look on his face. I got out of my Mustang and smiled tentatively, trying to be friendly.

Hutch's face turned from surprised to guarded. "Hey, there," he said. "It's been a long time."

I nodded and stuck my hands in my pockets. "It has, yes." I looked around. "Rhett here?"

He thumbed toward the inside of the bay. "The office in the back."

But I didn't have to move. Grizz came out of the bay just then, emerging from the shadows with his gaze glued to me. Geez. He was terrifying.

I had no qualms about him. He wouldn't hurt me. But if someone didn't know him, they'd be justified in feeling a little fear. He was a scary dude.

And a jerk.

Grizz and I stared at one another. I couldn't tear my gaze away from his blue eyes as he slowly walked toward me. He was like a magnet, drawing me toward him even though I wanted to slap him rather than talk to him.

"You two are going to burn the garage down," Hutch said dryly.

That was enough to help me look away as my cheeks flamed red. "I need to talk to you," I said with my spine stick straight.

With a nod, Grizz turned and held his hand out. "This way," he said.

I walked straight to the back, to the only door that didn't have a bathroom sign on it. The interior was surprisingly clean and nice and cool.

"I told Rainer about you," I said stiffly after we sat down on either side of his desk.

His breath hitched in his throat. Was he really this emotional about a child he hadn't wanted? Could he have had that much of a change of heart?

"Rainer wants to get to know you, but we both want to take it slow," I said. "I'll allow you to talk to him, but I need you to promise me that you actually do want to be a part of his life. For now and forever."

Grizz straightened up and he'd been looking hopeful and happy. Now he just looked pissed. "I'm no deadbeat."

I cocked my head and lowered my eyebrows, giving him a pointed look.

He held up his hands, his face getting redder. "Hey, I didn't know. My absence wasn't intentional."

I gritted my teeth and fought to keep my cool. I should've done as Aunt Patty said and done some screaming there. "You didn't give me the benefit of the doubt after a summer of me being totally hung up on you. You knew you had me wrapped around your finger," I snarled. "And you just dismissed me without a second thought."

He opened his mouth to try to defend himself, but there was no defense.

"No," I said sharply. "You won't railroad me when it comes to Rain. I won't feel guilty for not coming back when you clearly didn't believe me the first time."

Being around this man was totally draining, and he frustrated me down to my soul. How in the world had I allowed him to charm the literal pants off of me back then?

I stood and flipped my hair off my shoulder. "We'll be at Greenway Park on Saturday after lunch. I signed Rain up for baseball. I'll let you come, because my boy is wonderful, and he deserves everything in life, including a dad."

After walking away, I stopped at the door. "Don't let him down," I said quietly without turning around. "Don't you dare." With that, I walked out of the bay, nodding to Hutch, and got in my car.

I wanted this to work out, but only for Rain. It was all about him. Anything I ever felt for Grizz was dead and gone.

I'd never fall for his charms ever again.

Chapter 7 - Grizz

I looked across the table at Hutch, not able to comprehend what he just said.

"Define missing," I said.

Hutch shrugged and stood up to pace around the compound. I was thankful we were the only ones in the big ancient warehouse. I didn't want anyone else hearing Allen brother business. This was family stuff, not for the rest of the clan or gang to know about.

Hutch leaned against a wall and looked at me. "Big brother, I don't really know how to make it much clearer. Missing in action, MIA, off the reservation, do I need another cliche?"

I didn't like his tone but let it slide. "So Reck has been off the grid for three days, and I, the fucking Alpha, am just now hearing about this?"

Hutch bobbed his head back and forth. "Well, yeah. But in my defense, he does dumb shit all the time. I figured he'd gone off with some piece of tail he'd found at a bar, or maybe headed up into the mountains to do some hunting. *I* didn't actually get worried until I couldn't get him on his phone this morning. Asked around, and nobody'd seen him for a few days."

I looked at Hutch for a minute. Worry had wormed its way into my head. "You think he went to pull a job on his own?"

Hutch chuckled. "Well, if he had something planned, he did a damn good job of keeping it a secret. He also did it by himself, or has gotten some new boys together for his own gang. Not one member I talked to had any clue where he was."

I ran my hand over my face and through my hair, without looking back at Hutch. "You know he's gonna get himself killed one of these days. I mean, there's a reason we have the clan and the damn gang. He has all the help he would ever need. He's too fucking wild. When I nicknamed him Reck, I thought it was cute, you know. He was only seven when I did it. I really thought, like, one hundred percent believed, he'd grow out of it."

Hutch said, "Bro, I wouldn't worry too much about it. I mean, he's a grown-ass man. Can't really ground a twenty-three-year-old kid. We aren't really in the prison business, right? Hard to lock someone down forever. Maybe he just needed a breather. Took his bike on a little road trip. Maybe he headed south for some debauchery in Vegas for a day or two. Who knows, Grizz? I just wanted you to know he was gone."

I leaned back and put my booted feet up on the table, two loud *thumps* echoing around the converted building. "You're probably right, but you and I know he's got to chill out at some point. He's gonna get in trouble somewhere down the line."

Hutch burst out laughing. "Grizz, it'll need to be something big to get Reck to slow down. He only knows one speed in life. I mean, he even rides fast bikes. He rides that shitty Japanese sport bike, for fuck's sake, instead of a man's bike."

I shot Hutch a wry grin. "He'd beat the shit out of you if he heard you disparage his crotch rocket."

"The little shit can try," Hutch shot back.

We both laughed and Hutch walked over the fridge that sat near the old roll-up garage door. He pulled out two bottles of beer and handed one to me. I popped the top off and took a long swig. Swallowing, I saw that Hutch was looking at me with a weird little grin.

Exasperated, I asked, "What?"

Hutch said, "Well, I heard you and Zoey in the office the other day-"

"Oh, for fuck's sake!" I said, cutting him off.

Hutch raised a hand, gesturing for me to calm down.

"Now hang on, just hang on. All I was going to say was that your, I don't know, *conversation*? Got a little heated. She's not the kind to piss off is all I'm saying. You can poke a bear all you want, but be careful poking at the mama bear. That shit usually doesn't end well."

I gritted my teeth. I was embarrassed and a little ashamed. I was supposed to be calm, collected, all the things an Alpha should be in intense moments like that. But Zoey? I didn't even know how to handle her anymore. She wasn't the same girl from years ago. When I'd first met her, she would blush if I'd just looked at her. Now? She was fierce as hell. It was almost scary how mad she'd gotten, yet she kept herself under control. I'd been able to smell the fury on her, coming off in waves. Hutch was right, she *was* a mama bear, ready to tear me apart if I did anything to hurt Rainer.

Sighing, I said, "Just—just keep your damn ears to yourself next time."

Hutch took a quick pull from his own bottle. "Hey, my ears are only half the problem. I saw her storm out. She was...whew...bangin' hot! Some women are like that, the angrier they get, the sexier they are."

I cut my eyes over to him, a low rumbling growl rising up from my throat, a challenge.

Hutch chuckled. "Easy, big bro, just fuckin' with you. It's true though. That chick is capital G gorgeous!"

Unbidden, a mental image of Zoey flashed across my mind. Hutch was not wrong. She was even more beautiful than she'd been years ago.

She was the exact type I usually went for. The curves, the hair, the eyes? Good lord! One problem. She damn well seemed to hate me. Honestly, I didn't blame her for that. After the argument the other day, I didn't think she'd spit on me if I'd been on fire.

Hutch chucked his bottle into a trash can. "Anyway, you still plan on going to the game Saturday?"

I nodded. "Plan on it. I have to take every chance I can get to get to know Rainer. I mean...I've got a lot of time to make up, right?"

Hutch made an ironic face. "Uh, yeah. That may be an understatement. You good going by yourself? Need any...what do they call it? Moral support?"

"No, I'm a big boy. Besides," I said, "I have to get to know him pretty well before introducing him to the pack."

My boy, I thought again for the thousandth time since seeing him. *I've got a son.* I just wanted to haul him in, and let everyone see how strong and brave he was. Hell, I hadn't even gotten to know him yet, and I was dying to show him off. I was already proud of him. It was a weird feeling.

There was no way Zoey would let that happen yet though. I had to take things slow. Especially after that little blowup we'd had.

But that didn't matter. I didn't care. I would go as slow and steady as I needed to for my son's sake.

***

Saturday came, and I was anxious as hell. The game was in the afternoon and the whole morning leading up to it was like a dream. I couldn't even remember what I did all day to kill time. Suddenly, I found myself at the ballpark, flipping down the kickstand of my Harley. The smell of the grass, most times a pleasant scent, seemed stronger than usual, almost acidic. It was my nerves messing with my senses.

After putting my helmet on the seat of my bike, I walked over to the fence surrounding the field. There was a huge group of parents on one side watching the kids warm up. I strayed to the far end, no desire for small talk with people I didn't care about. I didn't even think to look for Zoey. At that moment, my eyes were scanning all the boys. Looking for him. It didn't take long.

Rainer was, for want of a better description, a spitting image of me. The black hair, the cheekbones, even the eyes! It was like looking in a mirror.

My heart made a weird trippy hammer, kind of like stomach butterflies, but in my chest. A smile started to break out on my face as I watched him throw a ball to another boy. The kid had one hell of an arm.

The smell of vanilla, jasmine, and the clean scent of rainfall hit my nose. Zoey. Only one person on Earth had ever smelled like that. I didn't turn around, knowing she was coming up behind me.

"I didn't tell him you were coming," Zoey said as she leaned up against the fence next to me. "Didn't want him getting even more nervous about his first practice."

I nodded, finally pulling my eyes from Rainer and locking them onto Zoey, "Yeah, no, I get it. The dad you never met is gonna watch you at your first ball game?"

Zoey grinned at me. "Basically. Also, Rhett, I just wanted to apologize for the other day. I shouldn't have been so harsh."

I shrugged and said, "I deserved it. I was more of an asshole than you were."

"I'm glad you can admit that," she said.

I ignored the playful dig and nodded out at Rainer. "He's a real good-looking kid. Handsome as hell."

Zoey barked out a laugh that made me frown. I was worried I'd said something wrong. Though, her laughter didn't seem bitter or angry.

"You would say that, Rhett! He looks just like you."

I couldn't help but grin. "Well, I'd say he looks a hell of a lot more handsome than me."

She rolled her eyes at me and tugged at my leather jacket. "Come on. Let's get a seat."

I followed her to the bleachers, physically feeling the other parents eyeballing me. I'd tried to clean up, but I knew I looked like a rough asshole. Which, I guessed I really was. Zo sat us near the front to get a good view of Rainer when his team was up to bat.

I felt awkward sitting there, not talking, so I started with the first thing that came to mind.

"So, you know the same thing happened to Dax, right?" I asked, totally betraying my friend's secret. Well, it was out now.

Zoey looked at me blankly. "What?"

I winced. How the hell would she know Dax? I was being stupid, too nervous for my own good.

"Sorry. Dax is a member of the gang. He's a shifter too. After I saw you again, after all that time, I went and talked to him. He's the oldest of us, so I figured if anyone would know of something like..." I gestured toward Rainer. "This happening, he would know. He told me that he had a kid with a lady he met in Boise. A human woman."

Zoey's eyes widened in surprise. "Are you serious?"

I nodded. "Hutch and I just about hit the floor when he told us. He said he was nervous about the government trying to take his baby girl, so he took her in. Things worked out fine. Dax took her underground. Made sure things were cool, and no word got out. No suits came around asking questions."

I watched a flash of anger erupt in Zoey's eyes, and knew I'd fucked up somehow.

"Are you saying you're going to take my boy from me?" she hissed.

Oh, shit! I'd done this all wrong. I opened my mouth to deny it, but she continued.

"Are you threatening to run off with Rainer and hide him with your damn pack?"

"Shit, Zo! No! Absolutely not!" I whispered, trying to stay as quiet as possible. I could feel eyes turning toward us though, with my extra senses. I didn't have to see them. Some humans could feel the weight of a gaze, but nearly all bears could. "Not in a million years, okay? I was trying to tell you that this isn't totally unheard of, though I didn't know it before about a week ago."

She stared at me, piercing my gaze with her own. She must've seen that I was serious, because the rage slowly faded away, and as it did, the muscles in my body relaxed. I hadn't realized how tense I was once she'd gotten angry.

"I'm sorry," I whispered. "I didn't explain that right. I can see how you thought that's what I was saying. I'm sorry. I'm just saying that if word got out that we made a kid? It wouldn't be good. My kind isn't supposed to be able to have kids with humans. If people knew, the government might get involved."

Now that she'd calmed down, Zoey was again watching Rainer warm up. Without looking at me, she said, "Rhett, I highly doubt the government doesn't know that this type of thing isn't an ongoing problem. You are all pretty damn...horny." I watched her blush as she said it.

I nodded grudgingly. "You're probably right. What I was getting at is I didn't want you to worry that Rainer was, like, the only one. There's a support system of sorts in place. I would make sure nothing happened to him...or you, for that matter."

Zoey sighed, and I could almost *feel* her relax more. Before she could respond, we heard the call to play ball from the field. Our attention turned to Rainer and his team. They were in the field first. Rainer was a shortstop, the glamorous spot, Derek Jeter reborn, maybe. I smiled thinking about that.

The kid was fast, and he had these amazing instincts that I knew I wouldn't have had on the field. At least it seemed that way, but then, I may have been a little biased. The very first hit bounced in the dirt and Rainer took a knee, scooped the ball and fired it across his body to first base. An out. I couldn't help myself. I jumped to my feet and clapped. Zoey jumped up and joined me, yelling his name.

Rainer scanned the crowd looking for her. I saw when he caught sight of me next to Zoey. His hand stopped mid-wave, hesitating only an instant before smiling and waving to both of us.

She laughed and waved back, calling to him, "Good job, baby!"

I glanced over and saw the way she looked at the boy. I could practically see the love glowing around her. So much love that it made my heart hurt. All this time. And I missed it. Every...damn...minute. It made me happy to see the way she looked at him, but it also made me feel like a little bit of an asshole, too.

Never again, I told myself, *I'm not missing anything else. I just can't.*

I wanted to tell her something, maybe ask if they wanted to go have lunch after the game, but before I could open my mouth, my phone vibrated in my pocket. I pulled it out. It was Hutch.

A knot formed in my stomach. He knew where I was, what I was doing. Why the hell would he call me here? I shook my head and hit *ignore,* then turned back to the game.

Rainer's team ran toward the dugout, and the other team ran out to the field. The phone buzzed again. I pulled it out and it was still Hutch, calling again.

"Damn," I whispered and answered, shooting Zo an apologetic look. "Hutch? What the hell, man? You know—"

Hutch cut me off, "Grizz? Ah, man, I'm sorry, so fucking sorry. I know you're at the game but I need you at the compound. Like, right now!"

I had never heard Hutch like that. He sounded like he was crying. The hair on the back of my neck and arms rose up.

I said, "Hey, slow down! What is going on?"

Zoey was openly staring at me now with confusion and worry on her face. And a little irritation.

"It's Trey, man. He's here. It's bad, Grizz, real bad!" Hutch said, still distraught.

"How bad, for fuck's sake?" I asked, already stepping down off of the bleachers. Hutch had used Reck's real name. He hadn't called him Trey in over fifteen years as far as I knew. It had to be bad. I felt nauseous all of a sudden.

Hutch said, "Bro...I...I don't think he's gonna make it. Jesus, Rhett, get your ass down here!"

Hutch hung up on me. I stared at the phone for a few seconds as a whimper tried to escape my throat, but fought it back. Zoey put her hand on my back.

"Hey, what's wrong?" she asked.

I couldn't tell her. I realized it in a half second. It could be just the thing to cut me out of her life, of Rainer's life, forever. She was already so worried about my lifestyle, how dangerous it was. I couldn't tell her. In an instant, I made my decision, and I'd have to live with it.

I turned toward her, putting my phone away, and said, "Zoey, I am so sorry. God almighty, I am sorry. Something's happened. I've gotta go. Right now."

"Oh," was all she said. She didn't frown or get angry, but I could tell she was disappointed.

I was already starting down the bleachers. "I'll call you later, okay? Zoey, I truly am sorry. Please know that."

She just nodded at me and turned her eyes back to the game. "I'll tell Rainer. I'll make sure he knows it was something...important."

Oh, *fuck!* How the hell did I choose? My brother, who was possibly dying, or my son, who I hadn't even had a conversation with yet. In the end, I didn't have any words left to say, and time felt like it was running out.

I got to the bottom of the bleachers and jogged over to my bike. I swung my leg over the seat, and buckled my helmet, forcing myself to move slower than I wanted to. I kicked the Harley to life, the thick rumble coughed out, making everyone turn and look. Then, I glanced back at the field one last time. Rainer was up next to bat, but he was looking at me. He could see that I was leaving, and I watched his tiny shoulders slump just a little. I'd broken my boy's heart already.

What a piece of shit was I. I felt like I'd been punched in the gut. I spun the tail of my bike around and sped out of the parking lot, tears stinging my eyes as I went.

The trip to the compound seemed to take both hours and seconds. Time was working weird in my head. Thinking about Rainer, worrying about Reck, trying to figure out how to make it up to Zoey. Before I knew it, I was there, slamming the door open and running down the hall to

Reck's room.

Doc was there, working on him. Jesus, there

was so much blood. Hutch stood off to the side, a

bloody hand pressed against his mouth as he

watched Doc try to tend the wounds.

Doc turned his head and saw me. "The

boy's bad, Grizz."

"What the hell happened to him?" I asked,

stepping over to look.

"Stabbed, several times. I think...I think they

caught his kidney and maybe one of the lungs too.

I'm good with stitching up, bandaging, I can even

pull a bullet out if the case calls. But this? I ain't

that kinda doc, you know?"

I nodded at him.

Doc looked lost. "We gotta call an ambulance. Right this minute."

Hutch spoke up at last. "But we can't! Government boys will find out. We're supposed to stay low, stay quiet. Don't draw attention. Can't go to a hospital."

I waved a hand at Hutch. "I don't give a shit! My baby brother isn't dying on some dirty-ass table in this dirty-ass building."

"No." Trey's voice was wet and close to a whisper, but we all heard it.

I turned and looked at him. His eyes were locked on mine.

"Just let me die. If you keep me around, I'm just going to cause more Reck. You all will be better off without me. That's why you nicknamed me that, right?" He laughs at that, but the laugh turns to a cough, blood bubbling out of his lips.

I leaned down and took one of his hands, slick with blood. I looked over at Hutch ready to argue more, but he was already on the phone, talking to the 911 operator, giving the address.

I looked at Trey and said, "Look, baby bro, you can't die, because I'm not gonna let you. You hear me? I'm the Alpha, and what I say goes. You die on me without my say-so? I swear to god I will bring your ass back just so I can really kill you myself."

Trey laughed again and his eyes slipped closed.

"No!" I shouted.

I slapped his cheek hard, getting him to open his eyes again. Trying to keep him awake. Doc and I both stayed at it, keeping him alert, barely, for nearly ten minutes until the EMTs got there. When Hutch showed them in, the two men glanced around the room, a little shocked seeing the blood and the guns hanging on the wall. To their credit, they didn't say anything, but immediately started work on Trey. Doc stepped aside, looking grateful to not be in charge anymore.

I had to give one of the EMTs a hard look to get him to let me ride with them to the hospital. The whole way there, I held Trey's hand and did the one thing I'd never been the type to do. I prayed. I prayed hard as hell.

Three hours later, the entire gang was at the hospital. I sat on a chair, Hutch beside me, waiting for the surgeon to tell us the news. Even in my despair, I knew two hospital security guards had positioned themselves at the back of the room, watching the boys with keen eyes.

I'd never seen the crew look so down. Everybody was tense, and I thought everyone else could feel it too.

Even sitting there, wondering if my brother was going to be all right, I couldn't stop thinking about the way Rainer had looked at me as I sped off. I had hurt him, and I felt like shit for it. Now even more so. This day had to have been one of the worst in my life. The deaths of Mom and Dad being the only thing worse than this.

Movement caught my eye, and a small woman came walking briskly down the corridor toward us.

She stepped into the waiting room. "Mr. Allen?"

Hutch and I both stood and stepped over, not knowing which one of us she meant. She nodded to us and looked down at her chart. "I was able to close the wounds in his abdomen and chest. His right lung collapsed but he's got a chest tube, so we're fine there. He's incredibly lucky none of the wounds nicked an artery. We did have to remove his right kidney. It was too damaged. It will be a long and slow process, even for a shifter, but I think he's going to pull through."

The waiting room erupted into cheers, everyone hearing the news. Hutch and I smiled and shook the surgeon's hand, thanking her over and over. A massive weight had been pulled off of my shoulders. I'd never been so relieved. A couple of tears slid down my face after she turned to leave us.

I walked around the room hugging everyone, laughing about all the shit we were going to give Trey for almost getting killed. Through all that though, I could only think about one thing now that I knew he was safe. How the hell I was going to make things up to Zoey and Rainer?

Chapter 8 - Zo

"How you doing, buddy?" Kim asked Rainer. "You seem quiet."

He'd never brought up Grizz bailing on his game, so I hadn't either. No way I was talking about it to try to explain why he'd left. I wouldn't have gotten so upset if Rainer hadn't seemed like he wasn't that excited about winning afterward. That was absolutely because his father had left.

To his credit, Grizz really had seemed freaked out about something, but was this the life I was going to be putting Rain into? Drama and danger? I couldn't do that.

He had to have a shifter presence in his life, I knew that. But we'd do it on my terms, on my turf.

Rain shrugged at Kim. "I'm fine," he said with a hint of sullenness in his voice.

Kim gave me a significant look. He was not fine.

We sat around the kitchen table, eating hot dogs we'd grilled for family day. We'd been doing this for years, me and Rain, including any family who happened to be nearby, whether it was my parents or Kim if she was in town. Now that we were in Forest Heights, that meant Kim and Aunt Patty.

Damn Grizz. He might've legitimately had to leave, but his lifestyle was what led to the abrupt departure, I was sure of it.

"I'm sure he left because he had to get somewhere," Kim said.

I pursed my lips at her when Rain's head swung up to stare at us. "You think?" he asked.

Sucking in a deep breath, I looked down at my son. "I know so. He got a phone call in the middle of the game and had to run. It sounded like an emergency." I gave Kim a significant look. "And that's why I'm not mad at Rhett." But still, he hurt Rain, so I wasn't exactly *not* mad at him, either.

"Want another hot dog?" I asked, holding up the plate of wieners.

Rain, normally a human garbage disposal, shook his head. "No, I'm good."

Patty, Kim, and I exchanged a glance over Rain's downturned head. "Rain, would you like to pick out a movie to watch tonight?" Patty asked. "It's supposed to rain, so we can't go outside." She loved to wheel out onto the porch and watch him play.

He shrugged. "I can, I guess." Watching him push his beans around on his plate, my heart clenched. He'd never known rejection.

"Honey, how about sundaes after this?" I asked. "We still have the stuff for it."

He shrugged.

Leaning over, I put my hand on his shoulder. "You know you can talk to me about anything, right?" I asked.

For the first time in his life, my sweet little boy blew up at me. "I'm fine, okay?" He glared around the table at us. "I wish everyone would just leave me alone."

Almost immediately, his angry face turned to shock and tears filled his eyes. "Oh, I'm really sorry," he mumbled as he fought the tears. He looked scared as he stared at me, silently begging me to help.

I rounded the table and pulled him into my arms. "It's okay, honey."

He began to cry in earnest. "I'm so sorry, Mommy, I didn't mean to yell at you."

Rubbing his back, I looked over his head at Kim and Patty, who both looked like they wanted to pull him into their arms and comfort him, too.

"Sweetie, it's okay."

Kim held up her hands like claws and roared silently. It was the bear in him starting to come out. He'd have moments of angry outbursts. There was no avoiding that. Things seemed to be escalating quickly now that we were back in Forest Heights.

Could it be the vicinity of the pack? Maybe being near his kind was making his bear side want to make an appearance. Or maybe it was a coincidence and it was just time.

I wiped his tears. "It's okay. You're just going through some changes. It's a part of growing up."

He furrowed his brow and hiccupped. "What kind of changes?"

What to tell him? I couldn't keep it from him forever. People were going to figure it out soon if they hadn't already, with Grizz coming to the game. And people liked to talk. Damn small-town life.

"Honey, Grizz is a shifter."

Rainer stared at me like I was the dumbest person on the planet. "I know, Mom."

"How?" I exclaimed. "I wanted to be the one to tell you."

"One of the guys at the game told me that he's called Grizz because he's a grizzly bear." He shrugged. "It's okay."

"Do you know what that means for you?" I asked.

He shook his head, but then slowly his shake turned into a nod. "I'm going to be a shifter, too?" he whispered.

"Yes, baby," I whispered. "I think that's why you got so angry just now. Your bear side is gearing up to come out. You'll probably go through some changes as your body prepares to become a bear."

He looked up at me and grinned. "That's kinda cool. A bear?" He made claws with his hands the way Kim had just moments before and roared at me.

We all let out a collective breath of relief. He wasn't freaked out. Of course a little boy would think it cool to turn into a big, bad bear.

Rain ran around the table to roar at Kim and Patty, who laughed and hugged him. But then he froze. "Grizz is here," he said simply and ran for the door.

"Wait," I called. "Don't open the door. How do you know?"

He stopped with one hand on the doorknob and the other on his nose as the doorbell rang.

I threw up my hands and rolled my eyes. "Fine. Answer it."

Rainer opened the door on a very rough-looking Grizz. He needed a shave and had big bags under his eyes. It didn't escape my notice that he had the same gray AC/DC shirt on that he'd worn to the game yesterday.

Or that there was blood on it.

I stepped forward and pulled Rain back. "Hello," I said cautiously. "Are you okay?"

Grizz rocked on his heels. "I just wanted to stop by and apologize about yesterday." His gaze was glued on my son.

Our son. Ugh. I'd have to get used to that.

"Sorry, Rainer," Grizz said. "I wanted to hang out after your game, maybe take you out, but I had an emergency with my little brother I had to deal with. But it's all okay now."

He looked up at me. "I couldn't get his face out of my head when he saw me leaving. He'd looked so disappointed. I was going to ask your permission before apologizing, but he answered the door." He gave me a sheepish grin.

Wow. He was going to ask my permission, huh? That was a good sign that maybe he was going to try to do this thing the right way.

"You're tall," Grizz said to Rain. "But I'm six-five. I guess it's to be expected."

I looked down at my son and realized I was barely looking down. When *had* he gotten so tall? He'd be surpassing my own five-seven soon.

"You're probably going to have some extra growth spurts," Grizz warned. He flashed his eyes up to me. "Uh, does he know...?"

"He knows you're a grizzly," I said. "Only just a few minutes ago, though."

Grizz nodded, still standing on the porch. I wasn't quite ready to invite him in. This was all happening so fast.

I sighed. "He had an outburst at lunch. Of anger like I've never seen from him."

Grizz nodded gravely and looked around.

"Can we talk?" he asked Rain, but also glanced at me with questions in his eyes.

"Yeah, we can sit on the porch," I said. "Now's as good a time as any."

"It is family day," Rain whispered.

Oh, geez. Now he had to get all sentimental.

Grizz sat on the steps and Rain joined him. I sat on the rocking chair not far away to give them a moment. A well-supervised moment.

"Do you know who I am?" Rhett asked.

Rain nodded.

"I'm really sorry I bailed on you yesterday," he said. "I promise I wouldn't have if it hadn't been really important."

Rainer shrugged. "It's okay. I understand."

"We can talk sometime," Rhett said. "And talk about some of the changes you're feeling, and the things your body and emotions are going to go through in the next few weeks and months. Would you be okay with that?"

Rain nodded and looked up at his father. "Are you *really* a grizzly bear?" he asked.

I bit back my chuckle as Rhett smiled. "Grizz would be a silly nickname if I wasn't, wouldn't it?" he asked.

"I guess so." Rain put his elbows on his knees.

"I'm going to talk to your mom about setting up some time for us to spend together, okay?"

Rain smiled. "Okay. It's nice to meet you." He jumped up and ran inside, and as the door closed behind him, I heard him roaring. Probably off to stalk Kim and Patty.

Grizz stood and moved over to sit in the rocking chair next to mine. "How did I do?" he asked, sounding a little vulnerable.

I liked that sound. He was willing to let me take the lead and give advice. "You did well," I said. "And thank you for keeping me involved and not trying to push me out."

My heart raced as he looked over at me with his big blue eyes. But that was foolish. Just because Rhett and Rain were starting a father-son relationship didn't mean I'd be starting anything with the man. He was still the same guy who fucked another woman while I watched, heartbroken and pregnant.

"So," he said. "When's a good time for you guys?"

"I take care of Aunt Patty during the week," I said. "We have a night nurse and a weekend nurse, though. We're free on weekends, but he has games every Saturday."

Grizz nodded. "Okay."

"You can come to the games?" I invited.

He nodded and stood, so I followed. "I'll see you Saturday," he said in a deep voice.

Grizz's gaze caught me in its web, and he stared down at me, then took one step forward, like he was going to say something important. But then he changed his mind and turned toward the porch steps.

His stare made my skin tingle. He used to look at me like that, years and years ago. When his focus was all on me, I'd always felt special and important.

Praying he couldn't hear my racing heart, I ignored the fact that he was still the most handsome man I'd ever met, even with stubble and blood on his shirt.

He left, driving a truck, and when he was out of sight, Kim came out. I knew without a doubt she'd been watching and waiting.

"Well," she said and sat in the rocker Grizz had vacated. "You look twitterpated."

I scoffed and sat back down. "Stop it."

Kim snorted. "You looked at that man like he hung the moon."

Shaking my head, I pushed off and set the rocker in motion. "I'm not a doe-eyed eighteen-year-old virgin anymore, Kim."

"No," she agreed. "You're not. But you are a mom who loves her son. And it's clear Grizz is already halfway in love with him."

She was right about that. I still wanted to be cautious, but it was obvious Grizz was thrilled to have a son. It made my heart ache for all the lost years. For the way he'd rejected me when I'd told him I was pregnant.

"You're not going to be able to resist him if he ends up being a good dad," Kim warned.

"Stahp," I said in exasperation. "I'm not going to fall for Rhett again."

And I damn well meant it.

Chapter 9 - Grizz

I was about to punch Hutch. He sat beside me in the truck, literally bouncing up and down. His nerves were all kinds of wound up about meeting Rainer. I'd held off as long as I could, but his patience had worn thin, and he'd basically begged me to go. It was like we were kids again, and he was dying to go do something with his big brother.

"Hutch, man, you gotta chill. Okay?" I said.

He nodded but continued to fidget nervously. "We aren't gonna be late, are we?"

I sighed and shook my head. "After the last game, do you think I'm going to take the chance of being late? We'll get there at least ten minutes before it starts. Just calm the hell down already."

I turned into the ballpark lot a few minutes later. Hutch had his door open and was walking across the gravel lot before I even had the truck in park. I got out and hurried to follow him as he scanned the field, looking for Rainer, but it looked like the boys were still down in the dugouts.

Zoey caught sight of us and waved. I finally caught up to Hutch and pointed Zoey out. On the way over, Zoey stood watching the field, waiting for Rainer to come out. She wore a fake jersey with Rainer's number on the front and the word

Mom printed on the back, I noticed when she turned to speak to someone going around her. She wore *very* short shorts, and I couldn't help but stare at her legs. As irrational as it was, I didn't want anyone else looking at them.

Just before we got to the bleachers, Hutch nudged me with his shoulder. "Bro, if you keep staring like that, you're gonna start drooling."

I growled and bared my teeth at him, but he only laughed and bounded up the bleachers to Zoey. Hutch shook her hand and leaned in to say something I couldn't hear, even with my ears, and Zoey burst out laughing. My guts twisted in jealousy. She hadn't smiled at me, not *really* since we'd met again. Not like that.

I couldn't really blame her, but it still made me feel like shit.

I got to them, and instead of smiling at me, Zoey nodded. "I'm really glad you were able to come, thank you."

The greeting, about as warm as day-old coffee, didn't do much to make me feel less like shit.

Before I could sit I heard, "Grizz!" from behind me.

I turned and saw Rainer out on the field waving and beaming at me. I waved, smiled back, and sat down, my heart full that my boy wanted to greet me. What a feeling. I glanced at Hutch, who stared across the grass at Rainer, his jaw hung open.

"Holy shit," he finally muttered.

I nodded. "Yeah, I told you."

"Dude, it's like a damn carbon copy."

I laughed. "Like I said. Yeah, I know."

Hutch didn't, as a rule, get really emotional. The other day when Reck was so hurt, it was really the first time I could remember Hutch getting choked up, at least since Dad died. And now, he wasn't crying or anything, but I could see a dozen different emotions rolling across my brother's face while watching Rainer. Sadness, depression, amazement, and love. My boy was so loved, and he didn't even know it yet. Reck crossed my mind then. He didn't know about Rainer yet, but I was sure he would react the same way Hutch was. We'd been a three-person family for so long. All of us were starving for something more, someone to share our lives with. Maybe having someone to look up to him would make Reck finally settle the fuck down.

The game started a few minutes later. Rainer's team batted first. While we waited for him to come up to bat, I decided to make conversation. Attempting an olive branch, I guessed.

Looking at Zoey, I asked, "So how's Rainer doing?"

Zoey looked back at me and gave me a questioning frown.

"Not just in general, I meant...he's getting close to puberty. His first shift will be coming soon. Any, like, mood swings? Outbursts? Stuff like that?"

Zoey's face softened and she sighed. It was about the weariest sound I'd ever heard and made me sad. I remembered how Trey, Hutch, and I had all been during the first stages. We had been, for want of a better term, little shits for about six months before our first shift.

Zoey swept a stray hair from her face. "He's had one of the outbursts of anger, yelling, stuff like that. I told you about it. Then he broke down crying because he felt bad about what he just did. It seems like it's exhausting for him."

I nodded. It was understandable. From everything I'd seen, Rainer loved his mom, and seemed like a very sweet kid. It probably tore him up to yell at his mom.

"He's not doing it willingly," I said. "There's just a lot going on inside. All the normal hormones, plus the bear stuff manifesting. It's a lot for a little kid to deal with."

Zoey nodded. "I figured that. I don't hold it against him, it's out of his control. Honestly, it kind of reminds me of teenage girls. I remember the tantrums and drama when I was that age. Not quite the same thing, but it helps me deal with it.

Really, the thing that is the craziest is how much he's started to eat! He's eating like a full-grown teenager, not an eight-year-old. It feels like I'm feeding a bear..." She stopped and laughed. "Which, I guess I am."

I smiled back at her. "It won't last long. There are a few things that might help. Can I tell you? I don't want to assume you want my input. I totally understand if you don't."

"No, it's fine. If it will help Rainer, I want to know," she said.

"Okay. I would say try to get him out of the house as much as possible. Being outdoors really helps. Being cooped up inside a lot just makes the bear inside feel caged. He's not technically at shifter age yet, but all his instincts are telling him to be out in nature."

I pointed over to Rainer, who was next up to bat. He was bouncing up and down on his toes, his eyes bright.

"See how he is outside? He'll feel more free, less constricted, fully alive."

Zoey nodded, understanding. "Yeah, that makes sense. We need to be outside more, anyway. It would be good for him even if he wasn't a shifter."

I bit my lip, trying to think of the best way to say what I wanted to say. Instead of being subtle, I decided to just put it out there.

"I'd be happy to take him out every now and then. If that's okay? Maybe just a hike through the trails?" I let her absorb the request. She'd be hesitant to let us have time on our own.

I knew she worked during the week, taking care of her aunt. I would've loved to have a little time to get to know Rainer. She thought for a long time, just watching Rainer take practice swings before his turn at bat.

I was ninety percent sure she was going to say no when she answered. "We can talk to Rainer about it. If he's comfortable hanging out with you, then I'm fine with you guys spending a few hours together alone. He *is* your son, after all."

For a few seconds, it felt like my body had filled with helium, almost like I could float away. It made me excited and nervous, but most of all happy. I smiled back at her and turned to watch Rainer walk up to the plate.

The first pitch was low and outside. He didn't even swing. The kid already had great instincts for the game. The second pitch was right down the middle. Rainer swung and made contact. It sounded like a shotgun going off. Hutch and I both jumped out of our seats cheering.

Hutch waved his hands, pretending to fan the ball farther. "Go! Go! Get out of here!" he screamed at the ball.

I laughed as the ball flew over the fence for a home run. I screamed my guts out watching Rainer run the bases, a look of shocked happiness on his face.

Zoey stood and cupped her hands around her mouth and yelled. "Show-off!"

She clapped and high-fived Hutch and some of the other moms and dads near us. Rainer looked so proud of himself as he rounded second. My heart hurt at how much fun this was. How amazing it was to see this boy doing these awesome things. I didn't want to miss any more. Not ever.

Rainer jumped onto home plate to complete the run, then smiled up at Zoey, and put two thumbs up. She smiled and raised her own thumbs back at him. I couldn't help but stare at her with the ache in my chest getting worse. She was such a great woman, an amazing mother. A terrible sadness enveloped me as I realized that I'd missed out on even more than I thought. Not only had I missed out on raising my own son, but I'd missed out on the life I could have had with Zoey.

An hour later, the game ended. Rainer's team won. He had a second two-run home run later in the game, and he'd thrown out what would have been a tying run at home plate. The kid was great! I heard his coach telling the kids he was taking them out for pizza to celebrate. The guy wore a shirt the same color as Rainer's team. On the chest the words "Coach Ethan" were printed in big white letters.

Coach Ethan made his way over to Zoey. "Your kid is amazing, Ms. Richards. You've done a great job with him."

I should have felt proud hearing that from Rainer's coach, but I could see the way this Ethan guy was smiling at Zoey. And the way he placed a hand on her lower back as he spoke to her. He was flirting, and not even trying to hide it.

"I'd love to talk more at the pizza parlor. Can I call you Zoey?" Ethan asked.

I'd had enough and stepped up behind Zoey. The coach finally noticed me. He smiled at first, but that disappeared from his face quickly. He noticed my vest, the bear symbol sewn on the chest, and the puzzle pieces aligned in his mind. He glanced over to Rainer, then to me, and finally back at Zoey.

It would've been impossible for him not to realize who I was. It was obvious I was Rainer's dad. I had no idea of the implications of that information getting out, but it was bound to, anyway. Unlike Dax, I couldn't hide the fact that my kid's mother was human. It wasn't like I could take him and disappear.

Zoey looked at Ethan, who backed away, swallowing nervously. "Umm...I'll just see you guys at the parlor?" He walked away without waiting on an answer from us.

Zoey looked at me and narrowed her eyes. "Do you have to be so intimidating all the damn time?"

I scoffed. "What? That dude? How is it my fault he's a pussy?"

She rolled her eyes at me as Rainer ran toward us. "Don't talk like that around Rain," she hissed. Hutch hung back, closer to the bleachers, giving us room.

Breathless, Rainer spoke excitedly. "Did you guys see? Did you see how good I did?"

Zoey hugged him tight. "You did so good! I'm so proud of you!"

Looking at me, Rainer cocked his head. "Grizz, are you coming for pizza?"

I glanced at Zoey. But she looked me in the eye, waiting for my answer.

I grinned, taking that as her permission. "Wouldn't miss it for the world, big guy!"

"Yes!" Rainer high-fived me before running back to the dugout to grab his bag.

Hutch slid up next to me. "I'm gonna head out. Give you time to get to know each other. We can do the whole 'this is your new uncle' bit later."

I frowned and looked around. "You rode with me. How are you getting back?"

"One of the boys is coming for me. I texted them about twenty minutes ago. Don't worry about me, just get to know your boy." Before turning to walk away, Hutch waved at Rainer. "Good job, kid! Helluva game, dude!"

Rainer, who was walking up with his bag over his shoulder, smiled and waved back, though he looked confused as to who the man was that was talking to him. Hutch disappeared into the crowd, and Rainer's attention moved over to my truck.

"Is that your truck?" he asked.

I nodded. "Yup, that's me."

"Can we ride in it? It's giant!" Rainer asked.

Rainer looked over at Zoey with big eyes. I let my gaze drift to her as well. Both of us were staring at her, hopeful looks on our faces. I rounded my eyes as much as I could, looking innocent and begging.

"Quit that! You guys look the exact same, with those big puppy dog eyes. Weirdos!"

Rainer grinned at that.

Zoey pointed at me. "He sits in the back, got it?"

I chuckled. "Of course he will. Where else would he sit since you're sitting up front with me?"

A blank look crossed her face.

"I'm taking you guys for pizza! I'll bring you all back here for your car later." I shrugged.

Zo grinned. "Grizz, that doesn't make any sense. The pizza place is all the way across town. You'd have to spend like an hour in the truck going back and forth and then home to the compound."

I held up my hand. "No, it's fine. It's a great day for a drive."

"Seriously, Grizz, it just makes —"

"I'm hungry! Come on! Let's go!" Rainer interrupted, letting me off the hook.

Zoey sighed and chewed her lip. "For the love of god, fine," she mumbled, then stomped toward the truck.

Rainer laughed and looked up at me. "She

never caves in so easily!"

He ran to catch up to her. They clasped

hands and walked together to the passenger side.

I couldn't take my eyes off them as they walked.

My heart was exhausted from all the emotions I'd

felt today. It was a great feeling to have.

Chapter 10 - Zo

The ride in the truck was... interesting. As soon as we were all buckled up, Rain started in. "Does it hurt to shift?" he asked.

"No," Grizz said, smiling at Rainer in the rearview. "It's natural for us. Like having a really satisfying stretch. There's no bone popping or muscle snapping. There's magic in it. Technically, shifting is a curse put on humans many hundreds, maybe thousands, of years ago. The magic helps us shift without changing clothes..." He winked in the mirror. "Although there's something freeing about running naked through the woods, then shifting into a giant, hulking bear."

Rainer thought that was absolutely hilarious. Naked jokes ranked up there with fart jokes with an almost nine-year-old.

"Do all shifters' children become shifters?" Rain asked next.

Rhett nodded without looking back this time. "Yes, as far as I've ever known. But there's no telling about humans. We have no idea what makes a baby work between shifters and humans, considering I only know of two in existence."

I poked him in the leg. I hadn't had any deep, informative talks yet with Rainer about sex. He knew about bad touches and the like, of course, but I had yet to inform him about parts A

going into parts B and that was how babies were

made.

May that conversation wait another couple

of years.

"But when will I shift?" Rainer's questions

were never-ending.

"Well, the youngest I've ever heard of is

eight. Most around age nine and ten, and the

latest up to twelve."

So any time now. No wonder he was having

mood swings.

"This is so cool," Rain exclaimed. "I can't

wait to shift."

His excitement nearly brought me to tears. He had no idea how his life would be different from what he expected. He was absolutely oblivious to the stark changes. He'd be shunted to the side, unable to grow and shine as he once would've. Shifters were supposed to stay to themselves, keep their emblems or logos visible so that humans always knew who the shifters were. It was the way the government had figured to keep shifters on more of an even keel with humans.

Not exactly fair to the shifters, who were often treated like second-class citizens, but it was what it was.

Except now my son would be a part of that shunned, private world. That fact weighed heavily on my heart. I turned in my seat and smiled at Rainer. "Honey, the thing is... People aren't always kind to shifters. Some people won't understand and won't like you being a bear."

Rainer furrowed his brow. "But people know Grizz is a bear. And they'll know he's my dad, won't they?"

Sometimes I forgot how observant he really was. "Well, people have never heard of a half-human, half-shifter. So, they may think it's a coincidence, or that Grizz and I are friends only. They won't know."

"For now," Grizz interrupted, "just keep it to yourself. That's the smartest thing to do. For now. It will make life easier on you. We don't actually know for sure you'll shift yet, so let's wait until we know, okay?"

Rainer nodded gravely. "I wouldn't want to lie." He looked worried for a second. "Do you think I will?"

Rhett winked in the rearview. "Yes, I think you will. But we can't be sure until it happens."

He perked right up, then. He was still young enough that the thrill of the shift trumped everything else.

I certainly hadn't expected to sit with Rhett the whole time at the pizza place. But as soon as we got there and claimed a booth, Rainer took off to play and joke with his new baseball friends. "I didn't expect him to be this excited," I said quietly to Rhett.

He laughed. "An eight-year-old boy who just learned he'll be able to turn into a bear? He'd be odd if he wasn't excited."

I thought for a moment and had to laugh myself. He was absolutely right. I did worry about my son, mainly because of how limited he'd be now, but for now, he was having the time of his life. "I worried I'd have to help him through this change on my own one day," I said softly.

Grizz reached over and touched my hand. "I'm very glad you came back. Now you don't have to do this alone, and now I get this amazing kid." He looked overwhelmed with his emotions as he locked his gaze on me.

I lost myself for a moment.

"Can I sit next to you, Grizz?" Rainer's little voice pulled me out of my daze.

Rhett started and then grinned at his little mini-him. "Come on, then." He scooted over so Rainer could climb up.

Watching them together, side by side, was a lesson in holding in my laughter. When the pizzas came, Rainer mimicked everything Rhett did. The way Rhett held his pizza, when he took a drink. Rain was Rhett's tiny, identical shadow. Grizz didn't notice at first, but when he did, it seemed to please him. After that, he watched Rain's every movement out of the corner of his eye and his lips began twitching as he also held back his amusement.

I didn't miss the stares from the others. Rumors were sure to be spread far and wide. I'd deal with them when they did.

"Excuse me." I looked up to find Rainer's coach smiling down at me. His gaze staunchly stayed on me, never straying to Grizz.

"Hello, Coach Ethan," I said with a smile.

"Could I speak to you?" he asked. "Alone?"

I glanced over at Grizz to find him glaring with his brow furrowed and the angriest expression on his face. What was with him? It wasn't like we were together.

"Sure," I said and scooted out of the booth, following Ethan to a booth across the room. "What's up?" I asked nicely.

Ethan sucked in a deep breath and crossed his hands in front of him. "I don't mean to be in your business," he said. After glancing toward the booth where Rain still sat with Grizz, he twitched his lips. "But I just couldn't help but notice how much Rainer looks like Grizz."

And here it was. I nodded once.

Ethan sighed deeply, like he was taking on the weight of the world. Or judging me for it. "I'm sorry to tell you this, but shifters can't play on human teams."

My good humor vanished in an instant as my back stiffened.

But Ethan didn't recognize the warning in my body language. He continued, "Shifter kids have an unfair advantage against *normal* children. Unfortunately, if Rainer is a shifter, he can't play on the team."

My jaw clenched and nostrils flared as I fought to keep my temper. It was true that bear shifters were a lot stronger than humans. And faster. They had keener senses of sight and smell, of course. But Rain was only beginning to develop his extra side, his supernatural side. He wasn't any better off than the other kids. "Rainer can't shift,"

I hissed as I looked around to make sure nobody

was listening too closely. "He's only eight. He has

no super strength or super speed. The only thing

he's manifested so far is a keener sense of smell."

I leaned forward. "He's just a kid, Ethan."

But Coach Ethan just shook his head again.

"I really am sorry. Those are the rules."

"Your rules are bullshit," I said, unable to

keep the anger out of my voice. Rain had made

friends on the baseball team already and now I

had to break his heart over something he

completely couldn't help.

"Are you okay?" Grizz appeared by my side, one hand on my back and his eyes looking worried. "What's going on?"

"No, I'm not okay," I hissed, controlling my volume again. "He's kicking Rain off the team. Because he's half-shifter." Tears had begun to roll down my cheeks, as much as I didn't want them to. Damn my emotions. I cried when I got angry, always had. It was the worst.

Grizz cupped my face and brushed the tears off of my cheeks with his thumbs. "Calm down," he said in a low growl. "I'll figure it out."

He slid in the booth beside me, one arm around me, and stared at Ethan. "The rules say shifters can't play, right?" he asked.

Ethan swallowed and nodded as if he was so sorry. But I hadn't missed his emphasis on normal.

"Do the rules say anything about half-shifters?" Grizz asked. "I don't think they do."

Ethan sputtered. "Of course they don't, because there's never been any such thing." He looked at Rainer, across the restaurant, laughing with a couple of boys from the team.

"Unless you change the rules so that half-shifters can't play, you can't exclude Rainer." Grizz leaned forward and lowered his voice even more. "Don't forget who I am. Don't forget who I know."

Ethan paled visibly.

Rhett continued, "If my son feels unwelcome for any reason, you won't be happy with the outcome."

Ethan paled further and swallowed, then looked at me. "I'm sorry," he said. "I was wrong. Rainer is fine and welcome on the team."

I followed Rhett out of the booth and looked around for my son... our son, but didn't see him. "Where is he?" I asked.

"I gave him a few bucks to take his friends to the arcade," he said as he motioned in that direction and put one hand behind me. "I sensed your tension."

I stuffed my hands in my pockets to hide how hard they were shaking. I wasn't scared or anything. More furious and full of adrenaline.

Grizz pulled me to the side in the hallway that led to the arcade, and I found myself enveloped in his arms with my head pressed to his chest.

Oh, wow. This was... a lot.

My fury overtook my mix of discomfort and pleasure at being in Grizz's arms. "How dare they treat him like that?" I asked. "I don't think I've ever been so angry." I pulled back but he kept his arms around me. "Did they give you a hard time as a kid?"

He rubbed the small of my back. "Worse, honestly. I wasn't a good kid like Rainer. I was a hellion *and* a shifter. I got a lot of shit. But shifters in general are given the side-eye, because people only see animals."

My hackles rose. "His life won't be easy, will it?" I whispered. My emotions threatened to overwhelm me.

"Easy, Mama Bear," Grizz said. I looked up into his smoldering eyes. "The way you protect our son is sexy as hell."

He stepped back and smoothed the hair off of my forehead. My heightened emotions, already in a total turmoil, went into utter confusion. The heat between us was intense. He closed his eyes, then put a foot between us.

"Make no mistakes," he said in a rough voice. "I'm feeling everything I believe you are. And I have every intention of making things right between us."

Do what now? I stared up at him with wide eyes.

"But this time," he said, "I'm doing it right."

We let Rain play until the other children began to leave with their parents. There were a lot of looks exchanged between us.

A lot.

Rainer always had a ton of energy, but it had been a long, eventful day for the little guy.

We got halfway back to my car at the ballfield and he fell asleep, immediately snoring like a freight train.

Grizz looked back at him while we waited at a red light. "Does he always snore like that?"

"Like a grizzly bear?" I retorted dryly.

Grizz laughed loud enough to wake Rainer up, but he dropped back off, his head hanging over the seatbelt, a half-mile up the road.

My stomach clenched in surprise and a little bit in desire a few seconds later when Grizz slid his hand across the truck seat and put it over mine. "You're not alone in this anymore."

I didn't pull away.

Why I didn't pull away was probably thousands of dollars' worth of therapy, but I'd have to do with telling Kim and Patty later and trying to avoid the shit they were sure to throw at me.

When we got to my car, Grizz transferred the totally conked out Rainer from his truck to my car and buckled him in.

"Will he wake up when you get home?" he asked once he shut the door to the back seat.

I shook my head and chuckled. "Nope. He sleeps like he's hibernating. I should've known he was a bear from that." I looked lovingly at my boy. "I can carry him, though. He's big, but not so big that I can't maneuver him in the house."

"Thank you," Grizz said softly.

"For what?" I looked at him in surprise.

"You've done a wonderful job with our son." He looked at Rainer through the car window with the same expression I imagined I had on my face. Devotion and love. "He's a great kid, and it's entirely due to you."

Whoa. That was pretty good. He was slick, I'd give him that. I had no doubt he meant it as a compliment, but all it did was make me want to burn my panties and drag him out to the middle of the baseball diamond and have my way with him.

He sensed my mood. Grizz bent a little and pressed a soft kiss to my lips, and of course, I didn't even remotely try to stop him. "You're bad for my health," I mumbled against his lips.

Laughing, Grizz cupped my cheeks again and stared down into my eyes. "Ditto. Can I see your phone?"

I pulled it out of my back pocket and handed it to Grizz. "Here you go."

He put his number in my phone, then gave it back. "Bye," he said softly.

As he rounded my car, walking toward his truck, he looked back at me. "Text me when you're safe at home."

I got in my car and went straight home. After wrestling my giant eight-year-old through the door and up to his room, I texted Grizz that we were home safe, locked myself in my room, and called Kim.

"Hey, bestie," I said when she answered. "I'm in deep shit."

"Why? What is it? Do you need me?"

"I think I do. I think I'm falling in love with Grizz again."

Chapter 11 - Grizz

The whole drive home, all I could think about was Zo. I hadn't kissed her in almost a decade, but those few moments back there? I was so turned on, I felt like a bear in heat, for fuck's sake.

She tasted sweeter than I remembered. Or maybe, it was just that I was taking it for granted back then. I was so stupid not to see what I could have had.

I spent the rest of the drive with my crotch throbbing, and my underwear uncomfortably tight around my erection.

Instead of going straight to my room when I got home, I detoured to Reck's. My brother still hadn't told us what had happened, and he hadn't been talking much either since getting back from the hospital. Doc told me he thought Reck was processing some trauma, maybe even had PTSD from the attack. Whatever it was, I wanted to make sure my little brother was okay. And I would destroy the people who did it to him. Once he felt like telling us.

I knocked on the door, a courtesy I normally only did because the last thing I wanted to walk in on was my baby brother with his dick out.

"Come in."

He was sitting up in bed, a book laid on his lap, "Hey, bro."

I grinned at him. "How's it going?"

Reck shrugged and lifted the book, "Got all this free time. Figured I'd catch up on some books I've missed out on."

I sat with him and pointed at the book. "What do you got?"

He looked at the cover and then said, *"Harry Potter and the Sorcerer's Stone."*

I gaped at him. "Reck, that book came out, like, twenty-five years ago."

He didn't seem fazed. "Yeah. Like I said, a lot of books to catch up on. Anyway, where have you been all day?"

"I'll tell you about it later. How are you feeling?" I asked.

"Decent, still sore as hell. I've never taken so long to heal before."

"You've never been hurt that bad before either." I stood up to go. "Listen, bro, you get some rest, all right?"

Reck shrugged, "Yeah, sure."

Once in my room, I turned the shower on. Zoey's taste lingered on my lips. Her scent and flavor weaved through my head, still. I felt like a kid again, kissing his first girl and then thinking about it for hours afterward. I stepped under the water and sighed as the nearly scalding shower rinsed the day away from me. My face directly beneath the spray, I was hard again. It had softened when I talked to my brother, but my erection had returned, aching and pulsing. All I could do was think about Zoey, the way her hair felt between my fingers, the way her body felt against mine. I couldn't stop the thoughts that filled my head, a fantasy that I wanted to fulfill. I closed my eyes and let my mind do what it wanted to.

Zoey was in the shower with me, soaping my body. Her hands slid across my chest, my shoulders, the suds building. She looked directly into my eyes as her fingers slipped across my stomach, then lower. I groaned as she circled her slippery fingers around me, moving them up and down my length several times before she let go, smiling.

I pulled her close, locking my mouth onto hers, our tongues gliding across each other. Her breasts moved across my soaped chest, nipples hard, tracing lines across my skin. I'd never been so hard in my life.

The water rinsed us as my hands explored her body, cupping her ass. She pulled away from me and went slowly to her knees, not taking her eyes off of me until she took me into her mouth. I gasped; I couldn't help myself. Zo's nails dug into my thighs as she moved me in and out of her mouth.

I couldn't take it anymore. I pulled her up and spun her around to enter her from behind. She raised herself up on my built-in shower bench, and I thanked my past self for installing it.

The sound of Zoey gasping as I filled her made me even wilder. Hungry, I reached around and grabbed her breasts as I started to thrust into her. My fingers gently pinched and pulled her nipples, my face buried in her hair. She whispered my name over and over as I went harder, deeper.

My world was going to explode in bliss. Zo arched her back and her hands went up behind her, fingers twining into my hair. Her hips slammed back into me, matching my thrusts. I was so close, my breath hitching, as I moaned her

name softly into her ear.

   Zoey groaned deeply, and shuddered under

my hands as the groan became a scream of

pleasure. As she finished, so did I. I buried myself

over and over inside her, ecstasy enveloped both

of us. Finally, we slid to the floor of the shower,

clutching each other, our mouths again finding

one another. This time it was a different hunger

that pulled us together.

   My eyes snapped open in the shower. I

stood there for a few seconds before shutting the

water off, my dick softening. I'd given myself an

orgasm with that fantasy.

   I sighed and whispered, "Well, shit."

The next day I woke to pounding on my bedroom door. I wiped my eyes and glanced at the clock. It was almost lunchtime. I hadn't meant to sleep for so long. I cursed and swung my legs off the bed and walked to the door to find Brick standing in the hall. Brick was about my age, his real name was Andrew something, but he'd been Brick for as long as I'd known him. He was one of the human members of the gang. I liked the guy, just not when I hadn't had coffee.

"The fuck do you need?" I asked wearily, still half asleep.

Brick looked nervous, bouncing and twitching. He was a little freaked out by something.

I huffed out a breath. "Come on, man, get on with it."

"I think I know what happened to Reck," he said anxiously.

My eyes widened, all thoughts of sleep gone in an instant.

"What do you mean?" I asked.

He wrung his hands. "I overheard some info. Do you want Hutch around to hear it?" he asked.

I bobbed my head once. "Yeah, grab him and get the rest of the crew together. It better be good, Brick!"

He grinned. "Yeah, I think it's pretty damn good."

I scrubbed my hands across my stubble.

"Okay, tell everyone to meet downstairs. Fifteen minutes!"

Brick ran down the hall, pounding on doors. I closed mine and got dressed as fast as I could. I didn't have any idea what he had found out, but I wanted to know soon. Reck's attack had gone too long without retribution.

By the time I got downstairs, most of the crew was there. Brick was whispering to Hutch as I stepped into the group. Hutch looked at me and made an angry frown. Whatever Brick had heard, it had Hutch pissed.

"All right!" I yelled, getting everyone to shut up, "Our boy Brick has some intel on who jumped

Reck." The boys all stared at me, their eyes hungry. It wasn't everyday someone tried to off one of the Forest Heights crew, and they wanted blood. So did I.

I nodded at Brick. "Tell us what you have."

Brick said, "I went to the barbershop in town to get a trim this morning. I went in my church clothes, you know? No leathers or anything, no way anyone would know I was in the gang." As a human, he wasn't required to wear our pack symbol. The shifters in the gang couldn't legally go out without the colors on. "While I was waiting, I heard a couple of dudes talking about some kid they roughed up. They were joking about all the holes they'd punched into him. Said they were surprised to hear he survived. Said it was fine, because he wasn't talking. I went to the bathroom to get a better look at them. They had Chaos Crew tats and patches."

A rumble of anger made its way around the room. My fingers tickled as my claws tried to pierce through my skin. Forest Heights and Chaos had trouble in the past, but it was always lame stuff. Never anything like this. They'd tried to murder my baby brother?

"Did you hear *why* they tried to take Reck out?" I asked.

Brick shook his head and chewed on a thumbnail, looking like he wanted to be anywhere but here.

"But," he finally said, "I'm sure they were the ones who did it. Just need your brother to confirm."

"All right, we'll talk to him," I said, glancing at Hutch. "Everyone else, just *stay cool.* Keep your eyes out, though. I'll let you know where we go from here."

I didn't wait for a response. Instead I grabbed Hutch and started toward the stairs. My brother followed wordlessly. Getting to Reck's room, I opened the door without knocking this time.

Reck was sitting on a chair staring into space, almost like he was stoned. He didn't acknowledge us coming in until Hutch snapped his fingers in Reck's face. Reck flinched and looked at us, terror in his face. A sudden, unexplainable surge of anger filled me and made me so mad to see him like this.

"Reck, we need to know what the hell happened to you," I said.

Reck only glanced at me and shook his head, then looked away.

I stomped my boot on the floor hard enough to sound like a gunshot. "Was it Chaos? Was it?" I shouted into his face.

The look of fear and horror on my brother's face told me everything I needed to know.

"Give me names," I hissed. "And I need to know why the fuck they tried to kill you."

Reck started to shake, shuddering like a dog afraid of a thunderstorm. It drained some of the anger from me. I looked at Hutch who was staring at Reck with the same bewilderment I felt. We'd never seen our little brother look so scared.

I put my hand on his shoulder. "You know who I am. You know I'll take care of it."

"That's the problem!" Reck yelled, tears slipping from his eyes.

"What?" Hutch whispered.

"*They* know who *you* are! They know who I am. They want you dead, so they can take the territory, okay? I'm...I'm not fucking important. I was bait, nothing but fucking bait. Kill the brother and get Grizz to retaliate. That's the whole damn plan!"

Hutch looked a cross between furious and nauseated. "They thought with you dead, Grizz would get reckless looking for revenge? Then they off him and take the spoils?"

Reck was openly crying now. "Yeah, okay? They want a war. I just don't want you guys to die. I...I couldn't take it! I was just in the wrong place at the wrong time."

I knelt down and put my hand on the back of Reck's neck, making sure he looked into my eyes. "They *will* pay for what they did to you. I'm not brainless. I've always got a plan."

I glanced up at Hutch and winked before looking back at Reck. "And I need to make sure you stay safe. My son needs to meet and get to know *both* of his uncles."

Reck was wiping the tears off of his face when I said it. It looked like it took a few seconds for my words to sink in. His eyes widened, and his mouth opened and closed like he was trying to say something, but the words wouldn't come. Hutch and I both laughed. He looked like a fish.

I gave him the quick rundown on everything that had happened. Nine years ago, Zoey, Rainer, the whole deal. Reck's tears dried and he smiled knowing he had a nephew, but then turned solemn a few minutes after the story.

"Grizz, man, if word got out you had a kid? I don't think Chaos is above going after kids, brother. They should be here at the compound. They need protection, right? Does anyone else know yet?"

Again, I looked at Hutch. His face had gone hard. He knew what I was thinking. Word was probably already spreading. Jesus, not only did I need to worry about the black suit government types, now I had to worry about some asshole gang coming for me and mine.

"I'll call Zoey. Hutch, you head out with some of the boys. Just keep an eye on her, okay? Her place, her aunt's, and her friend Kim."

Hutch nodded and was out the door in a second. I left Reck to rest, went back to my room and grabbed my phone. I hit the speed dial for Zoey. It rang three times before she answered.

"Hello?" she said.

My heart leapt into my throat. One more thing, another blasted damn thing that might scare her off. I could've lost her and Rainer because of this shit. And if she ran? Took Rainer? I couldn't even blame her. "Hey, it's Grizz."

"Yeah, what's up?" She sounded happy to hear from me. That was promising.

"I need to come see you, it's really important." I tried to keep my voice guarded.

"Uh, Okay. when do you want to come over?" Well, at least she was open to it.

"Now. Right now." I was already walking down the stairs and out the door, moving toward my bike.

"Oh, geez, um, okay. Yeah, we'll be at Aunt Patty's if you want to stop by." I'd figured she'd be there. She was supposed to be taking care of her aunt.

I sighed and said, "Okay cool. Be there in twentyish minutes."

"See you soon."

She hung up and two minutes later, I was flying down the highway, my hair whipping in the breeze. The whole ride, I kept looking over my shoulder to see if I was being followed, looked

through every passing windshield to see if I found

angry eyes staring back at me. It was an

exhausting ride, but I made it in only fifteen

minutes.

Pulling into her neighborhood, I spotted

Hutch and Brick on their bikes. They were far

enough away that Zoey wouldn't see them, but

they could see the front and back door of her

house. I nodded and rode past them and up into

her driveway.

She was outside before I had the bike

turned off with her hair pulled into a ponytail, her

glasses making her look so damn gorgeous. Like a

hot teacher.

"Hey, what's up? You look like you've seen a ghost," she said, coming toward me.

My nerves were shot and for a second, I completely forgot what I needed to say. I took a breath and pulled her to me. She didn't pull away, to my pleasure. Instead, she came willingly. I kissed her deeply, so worried about her that all I could think was that I needed this, needed her. She clutched at my shirt as we kissed. It went on for several seconds before I pulled away, leaving her looking a little dazed but in a good way.

"I have something really important to tell you. Where's Rainer?"

"Uh, he's at Kim's house. He's spending the night. Kim offered, just to give me a little break."

"Okay, good." After pulling her over to sit on the porch rockers, I told her about everything. The reason I had to leave the first game early, what happened to Reck, why it happened, and what it meant for us all. I felt like I was saying goodbye the whole time I talked.

She would refuse, I just knew it. She would probably be online buying a plane ticket before morning.

I tried to convince her before she could refuse. "I need to protect you all. I *have* to. My clan, my crew. If you let me put protection around you, I can promise you'll be safe."

She looked at me for several seconds, her brow furrowing as she considered the options. I steeled myself for her reaction. I knew, deep down, that this was it. She was gone. Rainer was gone.

Zoey sighed. "If you think it's best, then I won't argue."

I gaped at her, shocked.

She laughed. "I knew who you were before I allowed you back into our lives. I'm not some naive eighteen-year-old anymore. Your life is...well, violence is a possibility, right? If this means my son is safe, I won't fight it. Besides, keeping you from Rainer won't stop the rumors from spreading. There were dozens of people at the last game. There's no way people haven't started talking."

I kissed her again. "I was so worried you'd take Rainer, run away."

Zo sighed and rolled her eyes. "If I did that, I know I would regret it. He's already infatuated with you."

I looked into her eyes. "Is it just Rainer that's infatuated?"

She laughed again, but didn't say no. That was enough to put a smile on my face.

I spent the rest of the evening with her after shooting Hutch a text to let him know where Rainer was and to have a small group outside Kim's. He promised to take care of it, and Zoey called Kim to fill her in.

Once she settled her aunt in for a nap, Zoey pulled a laptop out and showed me hundreds of pictures of Rainer. From the hospital when he was born, to his last school pictures. It felt like I watched a hundred years pass by, seeing all the moments I missed. My heart broke a million times. "I'm so messed up about all the things I missed out on."

She smiled sympathetically. "You missed big moments, yeah. But there are going to be a lot more. Trust me, he has more life to live, and for the rest of it, he'll have his dad."

A lump formed in my throat. "I promise you, I'll be the best dad I possibly can be. I want my boy to have that. A man to trust and look up to, someone who is *there*."

Zoey looked at me for a long time before whispering, "I know you will."

I kissed her again, but this time I didn't pull away. Zoey's hand found my hair, and her fingers slid across my scalp, reminding me of my fantasy in the shower the day before. The kiss deepened, and we reached a tipping point. As much as I wanted it, *needed* it, I had to do this the right way this time.

Reluctantly, I pulled away. "I want to do this right, okay? Can I take you out on a date? A real date?"

Zoey smiled up at me, almost shyly. "Sure,

that would be nice. Really nice."

Chapter 12 - Zo

What a week. We'd made plans for our date for today, Saturday. Grizz had come and warned me that he'd put a protection detail on me, Kim, and Aunt Patty on Monday.

That left four days of worry about possible danger, wondering when Grizz would stop by—pretty much every day—and nervous excitement about my upcoming date.

By Wednesday, I needed a break. I left Rainer with Aunty Patty and her night nurse, nodded to the two guys on bikes at either end of the street, and headed to pick up Kim. She'd invited me to go out for dinner and decompress a bit.

Halfway through our appetizers, she set in. "So, what's up between you and Grizz?" she asked. "Do you still think you're falling in love with him?" She wiggled her eyebrows at me and ate a chip loaded with salsa.

I'd wondered how long it would take her to get to the point. "Maybe," I mumbled. "I feel so foolish like I'm repeating my past mistakes, but my heart is ignoring all the warnings my head is giving out." I moaned and loaded up another chip. Nothing like food to soothe the heart.

"Yeah, but it's pretty hot," Kim said. "And he doesn't seem to be the same guy."

I shook my head. "He really doesn't. Now that I see how he is with Rain, I do regret not talking to him more about the baby. None of us knew it was possible. I can see how he would think I was lying," I said. "Back then."

She scoffed. "Well, you better make sure he's not still screwing every piece of ass that comes into the club."

My heart clenched at the idea. "Yeah," I said sullenly before shoveling more chips and salsa in. "It's a constant worry." I wished I could trust that he wanted to be with me as much as he did Rain. "At least I do feel confident in how much he wants to be a father. Time will tell if he is consistent with it, but it's great for now."

"And if he hurts Rain, we'll kill him and hide the body so nobody ever finds it," Kim said with a shrug.

"Exactly."

Our food came, and we dug in. "I guess," Kim said around a mouth full of quesadilla. "All you can do is follow your heart one day at a time. If it's meant to happen, it will. Not fate, exactly, but these things sort of have a way of working themselves out."

I didn't know how much I agreed with that, but I didn't respond, because someone outside the restaurant window caught my eye. "Kim," I whispered. "Did your guards follow you to the restaurant?"

She paused with her fork halfway to her mouth.

"Act normal," I said. "Keep eating."

She took a small bite, then spoke with her mouth full, which didn't bother me, because we were both bad about doing it. "Now that I think about it, I don't think they were back there."

"Yeah, I can't recall seeing mine either," I said carefully as I looked down at my plate. "Keep talking and laughing with me."

I slipped my phone off the table, texting in my lap with one hand while I continued eating and keeping a pleasant smile on my face.

"I see him now," Kim said as she stabbed a piece of tortilla.

"Just act normal," I said as I texted Grizz.

At the Mexican rest on Coulter. Man staring at us through the window. Yours?

His reply came quickly. **Let me check.**

"Grizz is seeing if this is one of his crew, but if it is, it's someone I haven't seen before," I said with a bright smile as if we were having a fun conversation.

Kim nodded eagerly. "Good. Talking like this is freaking me out."

"Oh, he replied."

I set my phone on the table so we could both glance down at it and read. **Not one of mine. Do not leave that restaurant. We're coming.**

"Okay, then," Kim said. "We will sit tight."

Not five minutes later, I heard the rumble of motorcycles. So did my stalker, but he didn't hear it fast enough. He jumped on his bike and started down the road, but quickly found himself surrounded by Grizz and Hutch, along with several other men I recognized from the clubhouse or from hanging out on my street this week.

My gaze glued to Grizz as he got off his bike and stalked toward the man who had been watching me. He was so dominating. I wished I could hear what he said to the guy, but whatever it was, the man got the picture. He pulled his bike off to the side and a couple of Grizz's guys stood with him.

Grizz turned and walked into the restaurant, having zero trouble finding me. He made a beeline for our table. "Kim," he greeted. "Nice to see you."

Kim nodded with her eyebrows raised. "Hello, Grizz."

Grizz leaned over, staring me deep in the eyes as he pulled out his wallet. He threw a fifty on the table, which was far too much for the bill. "Come on," he said quietly. "Too many ears."

We got out to my car, and he boxed Kim and me in, blocking us from the road, but now that we were outside, it would be harder for anyone to eavesdrop.

"Things have escalated," he said. He handed me his phone. "Play that video."

I tapped the screen. "This is my house," I whispered.

"Keep watching," Grizz said in a deadly tone. Kim pulled on my arm and huddled close as we watched two of Grizz's guys dragging a man I'd never seen out of my house. "As soon as I started checking, I realized the group following Kim thought the group following you was staying here at the restaurant, and vice versa. Chaos must've been looking for an opportunity, and they took it. When I knew they had a man on you here, I had my guys at your house go in. They found this fool."

"Rain?" I asked, terror spreading in my gut.

"Rainer and Patty are fine," he said. "Dax is having tea with them and the nurse right now."

"What did you do with the guy in my house?" I asked in a whisper as I handed his phone back.

"Don't worry about it," he replied. "We didn't kill him, which was more than he deserved."

I hoped he hadn't done anything to my stuff, but I could worry about that later. Everyone was safe, that was what was important.

Sighing, he looked around before continuing. "Listen, the thing is, either you and

Rain need to come to stay with me, or I'm sticking to you both like glue until this is resolved."

I stared up at him, no clue what to say or how to do it.

"I'd feel better if you came to stay with me," he said. "Nobody's going to get to you there."

Reluctantly, and with a mind full of questions for how in the world it was going to work, I nodded. "Okay," I said. "Rain and I will stay with you." The compound was huge. We could just keep to ourselves, and I'd definitely keep Rain away from the debauchery that was inevitable there.

Things moved quickly after that. Grizz had

one of his guys go home with Kim. It was an older

man who remembered Kim from our time there

many years ago. She was going to put him up in

her guest room and help him find an unobtrusive

place to keep an eye on her while she was at work

at the daycare without freaking out all the

parents.

Grizz doubled the protection around Patty's

place, leaving Rain there while we settled

everything.

The next thing I knew, the sun had long

since set, and I was watching rough-looking men

carry boxes and luggage out of my house. Grizz

had asked me to pack whatever I felt would make

me feel more at home at his compound… so I had.

It was a lot.

Now that I saw it all being loaded into trucks and cars, I wondered if I went a little overboard.

Hutch had driven Rain over a little while ago on the back of his bike, which had nearly given me a heart attack in itself, but he'd delivered him with the promise that they'd gone super slow the whole way. And to be fair, it was a five-minute drive on neighborhood streets. It wasn't like they drove the Indy 500 on the way.

Rain stood to the side, joking and laughing with some of the guys. They all seemed so pleased to see him. For them to be such big burly bears, they all seemed to have a soft spot for my son.

I pointed to the last few boxes, then stopped and stared when Grizz came in, stooping low as he went through the doorway, because he had Rainer on his shoulders. Rain was laughing his head off.

One of the human members of Grizz's group—I disliked calling them a gang, though that was really what they were—was staying here at my house to make sure nobody from Chaos messed it up or broke in again.

"They were waiting on you," Grizz said when he handed Rain off to Hutch and we were the only two in the house. "Probably to kidnap you when you got home."

"That's why they watched me at the restaurant. To know when I'd be heading home." I closed my eyes and pushed away the revulsion.

"Is that everything?" Grizz asked.

I looked around at my stripped home. "I think so." It wasn't forever. Just until he settled this with this other gang.

Grizz loaded Rain and me up in his truck, and chattered with our son—*our* son—about his upcoming game. I let my mind wander until Rain changed the subject. "I heard one of the other kids' moms whispering about me," he said quietly. "At practice."

I twisted in the truck seat and stared at my son. "Who? What did they say?"

"She said it wasn't fair for me to play on the team since I'm a shifter," he said in a small, sad voice.

Suddenly, I wished I had claws. They would've been out and ready to attack this woman. "Who was it?" It was a fight to keep my voice steady.

"Jackson's mom," he said.

"Is mama bear about to come out?" Grizz asked quietly.

"You're damn right she is," I said, making my voice as growly as possible.

He just smiled. And it was a smile I would've liked to have seen more often.

We turned up a gravel driveway, following the line of trucks full of my and Rainer's stuff. "What is this?" I asked. "I thought we were going to the compound."

He gave me a puzzled look. "No, you're staying with me. I only stay at the compound now and then," he said.

I stared at the house in shock as the trees cleared and the whole thing came into view. "It's beautiful," I breathed.

Grizz's chest puffed a little. "Thanks. It belonged to my parents, and I bought my brothers out. They don't care about owning a home anyway, so it worked out."

The place was enormous, with windows absolutely everywhere, and a huge, white wraparound porch with big squared-off columns. "How much does owning an auto shop pay?" I whispered as I looked up. "Is that three stories?"

"Four, if you count the finished basement," he said. "Plus an attic."

Turning my head, I cocked one eyebrow at Grizz until he shrugged. "I don't just own the auto shop, you know?"

Oh, yeah. There was a lot I still didn't know. I sighed as he opened his door and ran around to open mine. "I'll tell you more on our date," Grizz said. "I promise."

Well, that was helpful, at least. If I knew what all he was involved in, I could make an informed decision about how far to let this go. "I figured the date would be canceled now," I said.

"No, all the guys are fighting to volunteer for uncle duties. But Hutch and Reck will kill them if anyone goes before them. Rainer will be perfectly safe."

As long as Rain wasn't around any of the parties, it was fine.

"Come on," he said. "I'll show you around."

The whole house was beautiful. Inside was sort of farmhouse meets heavy metal, but it worked somehow. Black picture frames, black trim. "Rain," Grizz called. "Come upstairs, I'll show you your room."

"His room?" I asked as I followed him up the big, wooden stairs.

"Yeah, of course. I started working on it this week." He stopped and grinned down at me. "I may have gone a little overboard."

Rain squealed and darted past us on the stairs. "Which room is it?" he yelled.

"Last one on the left," Grizz said. Rain took off running up the upstairs hallway, and we hurried to follow.

"Oh, Grizz, when did you find time to do this?" I asked as I walked in.

"I took Monday and Tuesday off. Once I was sure you were going to let me into his life, an idea for the room began to form."

The room was a little boy's dream. "Hey," I said sharply as he collapsed in front of an entertainment center that held a couple of brand new gaming systems and a fairly large TV. "The same rules apply here."

Grizz raised his eyebrows. "What rules?" he whispered.

"He's only allowed to play for two hours a day, and that's only if he's already played outside for at least an hour, done his chores, and homework."

He nodded. "Fair. I'll help with that."

The rest of the room was filled with baseball paraphernalia. "Is this signed?" I asked as I looked at a baseball in a clear, plastic case.

"Yeah, by Derek Jeter," Grizz said.

"No way!" Rainer ran over with wide eyes and grabbed the case off the dresser. "You remembered!"

"That he's your favorite?" Grizz asked. "Of course I did!"

Rain held it to his chest as he looked at his baseball-themed bedspread and curtains. I noticed the quality of the wood of the bed, dresser, and desk. The room was bigger than my bedroom at our house.

"This is too much," I whispered.

Grizz furrowed his brow. "It's not nearly enough. I've missed nearly nine years, not to mention how I would've liked to have been around for the pregnancy."

I cut my eyes at him. He could've been there for the pregnancy if he'd just listened to me, but that was old news. I needed to move on.

"Come on," Grizz said. "I'll show you our room."

Our room.

Our room. How had I not realized I'd be staying with Grizz?

"I don't have to stay in your room," I said quietly. "I don't want to put you out."

He stopped in a doorway down the hall, toward the stairs, then turned and looked at me in surprise. "Of course you're staying with me. The other rooms belong to Hutch and Reck. They stay here sometimes, even though it's my place."

He turned on the light, but then turned back to me again. "I don't mean to pressure you. If you don't want to stay in here, I can have one of them clear out space for you. Or you can stay in the basement, there's plenty of room down there to add a bed."

I considered my options.

Maybe I wanted to stay in here with Grizz. Would that be so wrong of me, to want to spend a little time with the father of my son?

"No," I said firmly. "I'll stay here."

Grizz puffed out his chest and showed me his closet. It was a huge walk-in—also bigger than my bedroom at home—and he'd cleared out half of it. A bunch of my boxes of clothes were already here.

I really had overpacked. I hadn't needed to bring *all* my clothes.

Grizz's side was full of jeans and black t-shirts. I chuckled and shot him an amused glance.

He just shrugged. "I'm a simple man." As he left the closet, he paused and glanced to his left. "Oh, right here behind this door is a safe room. Code is seven-four-two-four. If you ever need it, it's big enough for three or four people, though it's cramped. Now that you and Rain are here, I'll work on getting a bigger one."

I barely had time to see the inside of the small white box before he shut it. "Get ready. We're moving our date night up to tonight."

He didn't leave me room to argue, but after he'd gone to such lengths to keep us safe, he deserved one little date.

Of course, it was still his fault we were in this predicament, but that was a conversation for another day.

Chapter 13 - Grizz

I decided to take Zoey to the city for our date. Mostly to feel a little bit like getting *away* from everything that had happened the last few days. I'd almost said screw it when I saw her walk out of the bathroom. She'd put on this little black dress that almost had me on my knees. She looked so good I almost decided it would be more fun to just stay in. But, I had promised a date, and a date she would have.

I didn't ask her where she wanted to go, but I had the barest hint of a memory from back in the day. I'd taken her to a seafood place back then, and I remembered her loving it. So, I was taking her to the best seafood and steak house in Boise. When I pulled into the parking lot and saw her face light up, I knew that I'd nailed it.

"Oh, my gosh! I can't wait. Come on, let's go," she said. I had to hurry around the truck so I could open the door for her before she bounded out.

We got appetizers of fried calamari and raw oysters. I tried an oyster and didn't care much for it, but she blew through those while I satiated my appetite on the squid, which was really good.

"So, tell me about college. How did that go with being pregnant?" I asked, genuinely wanting to know.

Zoey put down the last shell and dabbed at her mouth with a napkin before she said, "I will admit, I got a few stares once I started to show, but I just ignored it though. I did my thing, studied, went to class, and rested. I rested *a lot*!" We both chuckled, and I wished I could've seen her. "My parents helped too. I really wanted that first year away from home, but eventually I had to move back. So I transferred from Texas to South Carolina University. Mom and Dad were my babysitters, my study partners, and my best friends through all of it. It was a massive blessing having them help me raise Rainer."

Wanting to know about my son's grandparents, I asked, "How are they doing? Are they planning to visit at some point?"

The server came and removed the appetizer plates and dishes while Zoey twisted her napkin in her hand and stared at the table, a sad look on her face.

"Um, Mom and Dad died about two years ago. Coming home, they were in a car accident. They both died instantly."

"Oh, shit, Zo, I'm sorry. I wish I'd known." I said sadly, feeling like an asshole for asking.

She smiled and brightened a little. "No, it's fine. You *couldn't* have known. It was really hard on me, of course. Still is. But Rainer was inconsolable for almost a year afterward. I put him in grief counseling and everything. To be honest, me coming up to Idaho to help with Aunt Patty was partly to get him into a new environment. Someplace he could start to come out of mourning."

She took a long drink while I gave her time to compose her thoughts. "It's really kind of ironic." she said. "My older sister died in a car crash too. She was a wild child. I idolized her, though. She was in all kinds of trouble. Probably would have made some bad decisions, and ended up in worse trouble if she hadn't passed away. I saw how her behavior and then her death destroyed my parents. So I played the goody two-shoes afterward. Did all the right things." She

paused and had a look like she'd just realized

something. "I guess I went too far to that side. It

almost suffocated me. Every kid is going to do

some dumb stuff, but I didn't let myself stray from

the straight and narrow *once.* Kind of the reason I

let myself…" She looked at me shyly, "do some

bad things up here that summer."

My own cheeks turned red. I hoped my

stubble covered most of it.

"But when I got pregnant, they never made

me feel bad about it. I could tell they were

disappointed, but that vanished once Rainer was

born. They loved me so much, and I think they

loved Rainer even more. To this day, it makes me feel happy. Loved, you know?"

"Yeah, right." I said, not really knowing. Mom and Dad had loved me and my brothers like crazy, but it had been a distant kind of love. Their love had been wound up in each other, so much so that I always thought that when mom died, it was that love, or the lack of her love, that killed Dad.

She clasped her hands together. "Okay, enough about me. Tell me, how are you able to afford that gigantic compound and the cars, trucks, motorcycles, *and* the house? It seems like you're pretty loaded. I just can't figure it out. Does the shop really make that much money?"

I shrugged. "I mean, we are a biker gang, but I moved us out of the old business a while back. I decided I wanted something more, ah, legal, I guess. I took some seed money and made a few investments. Silent-partner type stuff on some up-and-coming tech companies, crap like that. Found some kids that had a real fire, really fucking brilliant, and needed some cash to get started. A few of those companies ended up being multimillion-dollar ideas. So, I own between one and maybe ten percent of those companies. Don't go to the meetings or anything, I just let them use my seed money and now I cash the checks that come every month." I grinned, proud of how I'd invested my money.

"Some of the boys end up doing a few things on the side, little jobs here and there. But I make sure they all know not to go crazy, nothing overtly illegal. Really, they like knocking down drug runners, and stealing their dough, sending them home crying and scared to death to ever bring drugs around again. I let it go on because I look at that as a win-win. Technically, it's illegal, but it's fun. I'm a little jealous of them at times."

Zoey stared at me in bemused wonder. "No shit? Wow! I did...not expect that."

I chuckled. "You figured I had a whole Walter White meth operation running out of my barn?"

She blushed. "Well, I'd hoped not."

The entrees came out then. She'd ordered a seafood platter, lobster tail, crab legs, fried shrimp and a baked potato. I'd gotten a rare steak and crab cakes. Even after the appetizers, we were both still starving and dove in.

After a few minutes, I paused and cautiously asked, "So, how was your dating life before moving back?"

As she set aside a few crab shells, she said, "I've tried. A lot of the guys were great, some were assholes. None of them really stuck. We weren't meant to be. I was probably way too focused on school, on Rainer, on work. I had way too much going on to really be a great partner to someone. I just put it to the back burner and went on with my life. How about you?"

I took a deep breath, not knowing where to start. "I've never had anyone serious, not really. Just casual things," I looked at her. "My Mom died when I was younger, and I remember how much Dad loved her. He always joked that me and my brothers 'were the apple of his eye, but mom was the sun in his sky.' To this day, her dying broke my Dad's heart and I believe he died from it. It made me terrified to love anyone so much that they could break you."

She stopped eating and looked right back at me.

"I've had a pretty big change of heart though. There is someone out there that each of us is meant for, and they are definitely worth the risk." I couldn't be much more clear than that. Hopefully, she knew exactly what I meant.

The rest of the night went really well. We left an hour or so later and talked the entire ride home. I unlocked the door to the compound and we found Rainer and Hutch both passed out on the floor in front of the TV. There were Doritos and Cheetos bags everywhere. It looked like they'd eaten a half-dozen Little Debbies, too, from the look of the empty wrappers. Zoey had her hand pressed to her mouth to keep from laughing.

She shook her head and went to Rainer and picked him up. She was strong, 'cause he was a big kid. The boy didn't even stir as she walked to his room.

I nudged Hutch gently. His eyes sprang open, and seeing me, he yawned. He stood up and brushed chip crumbs off his pants. "Grizz, man, you've got a great kid. I'll babysit any damn time."

I laughed and patted him on the back. "Thanks, man."

Hutch walked to his own room and shut the door. It was a little late, apparently he was staying here.

Chuckling, I went up the stairs into Rainer's room and watched Zoey tuck him into bed. She brushed stray hair from his face, and I could see how much she loved him.

Zoey whispered, "I love you, baby, good night."

Rainer mumbled, half asleep, "Love...momma...night."

My heart wanted to explode. I knew that I wanted to love like that. That I *could* love like that. Watching Zoey with Rainer, it all came clear.

We went back to my room, and I started to get undressed for bed. Zoey walked toward the bathroom. "I think I'll shower."

"I can sleep over on the couch if you want," I said, praying she'd say no.

She just looked at me and smiled as she shut the door to the bathroom. I wasn't entirely sure what that meant, but it made my stomach do pleasant flips.

I stripped down naked and put on a pair of pajama bottoms, then I read for a few minutes until I heard the shower turn off.

Zoey came out wearing a towel and nothing else. She sat down beside me on the bed and started brushing her hair.

"You know, it's pretty damn beautiful what you and Rainer have," I said. "That type of relationship is amazing. I know I can't really take any credit, but I'm glad you're his mother. I couldn't have picked anyone better, not in a million years."

Zoey laughed. "Well, thanks for knocking me up, I guess."

I laughed along with her. I was glad we'd made up enough ground that we could both laugh about it, however uneasily. It made things feel less heavy between us. It made me feel a little less like the jerk I'd been.

I leaned forward and kissed her.

Zo kissed me back and let her fingers move across my stomach and abs. I moaned. She was so warm. I was already getting hard. Our kiss grew hungrier.

I pulled away and looked into her eyes. "We can take it slow."

She blinked back at me. "We've gone slow long enough."

With that, she pushed me back onto the bed and climbed on top of me. She pinned me down with another kiss, taking full control. Her tongue sliding into my mouth was the most erotic thing I could remember.

As I stroked and massaged, exploring her skin, her body relaxed under my hands. She was becoming pliant, ready for anything.

I was already panting, and I knew damn well she could feel me straining against my pants, pressing into her.

I let my hands loosen the towel. It slipped away with a whisper and fell to the side, revealing her body. My breath caught in my chest as I took her in.

She sat up, and the sight of her made me dizzy. Her full breasts were still flushed, pink from the shower. Her wet hair hung down around her shoulders, and a small rivulet of water wound its way down to her nipple and hung there. I leaned forward and gently licked it off.

Zoey gasped as I did it. I grabbed her butt and let my lips close around the nipple, sucking softly. Resting her head on top of mine, she slid her hands through my hair as I roamed my hands across her body, remembering her curves. It was like all the years had vanished, and I was back in that summer.

One of my hands left my hair and went behind her. She pulled my waistband down and pulled me free. Her fingers were somehow like fire and ice at the same time. I gasped as she began stroking me. I looked up and locked eyes with Zoey. I'd never seen a woman look at me that way, like I was the only thing she could see in the whole world. Not since she'd done it before.

I rolled her over and smiled as she giggled, sliding down her body, kissing her breasts, her stomach, the patch of hair between her legs. How could I have forgotten how perfect it felt to be with this woman?

Then, unable to wait and tease her more, I buried my tongue in her. Her body arched and she sucked in three quick breaths as I tasted her. I pulled her close, my hands digging into her thighs.

Zoey gasped a whisper out, "Please...please...now."

I rose up, again looking into her eyes, then pulled my bedside drawer open quickly, pulling out a condom and ripping the packet open with my teeth.

I rolled it onto myself and kissed Zoey again. While I kissed her, I slid slowly into her.

We moaned together as, inch after inch, we became one. I paused for a moment before moving in and out, prolonging our pleasure. She was already beginning to mean the world to me, and this, our joining together, made me want to be with her every day for the rest of our lives.

Her hands massaged my chest before moving up and wrapping around my shoulders. She pulled me close, and I rocked in and out of her, propped up on my elbows. I was a starving man and the only thing that could satisfy me was her.

Zoey bit my earlobe gently, and then whispered, "It's okay, I'm close...go faster."

I finally let all my inhibitions fall away, the last wall broken. We thrust against each other, nearly frantic with need. The final moment passed like a tsunami, unstoppable. She came first. Her back arched amidst a groan of pleasure. A few

moments and my own explosion of euphoria

made me shudder and sag, careful not to crush

her. Our lips found each other again as our hands

roamed across skin, curves, and hair. We fell

asleep like that, wrapped in each other's arms,

blissfully happy.

Chapter 14 - Zo

"Game day!" Rainer yelled from the hallway. "Everybody get up! We have to get to my game!"

Grizz moaned, and I rolled over, ready to tuck my head under the pillow, but he was right. I had to get up and get in the shower.

I must've dozed back off, because the next thing I knew, Rainer was in my face. "Mom, get up! We gotta go."

The poor fella had already dressed himself tip to toe in his little league gear. "Hey, buddy," I mumbled. "I'm coming."

"Mom." The urgent tone in Rain's voice made me open my eyes. "It's nine."

Oh, no! I jumped out of bed and squawked. "Get up, Rhett!" We were supposed to be at the ballfield at nine-thirty. "We're late."

I rushed into the closet. I'd just finished unpacking and organizing my clothes last night.

Rhett followed behind. "No time for a shower," he grumbled. "Feel free to wear one of my caps."

He pointed toward the corner, to a small rack.

I selected a small one with his auto shop logo on it, and pulled my hair into a ponytail, threading it through the hole in the cap.

We brushed our teeth in the double sinks in the bathroom, and slapped on deodorant, grinning at each other. I didn't know why he smiled, but for me it was because we were mirroring one another as we got ready. I'd never had that with a man, never had a partner like this.

I still hadn't resolved myself that this was fully happening, though Rainer had taken it in his stride. I'd intended to keep him from realizing I was sleeping in Rhett's bedroom, but he'd figured it out the first morning and never said a sideways word about it.

With a bit of hotfooting, we made it to the ballfield on time, partially thanks to Rhett being an amazing driver and going far faster than I'd ever have done. I had to make myself unclench and remember his reflexes and senses were far superior to my own. If anyone was safe driving fast, it was him.

"Go stand by the fence," I murmured when I spotted the infamous Jackson's mother. Corinne.

"Get 'em, Mama Bear," Grizz said as he realized who I was looking at.

I climbed into the bleachers. "Hello, Corinne," I said brightly. "May I sit with you?"

She nodded stiffly and straightened her spine. "Of course. How are you?"

"I'm well." I gave her a conspiratorial smile. "Just keeping an eye on my boy."

"Oh?" Her voice came out unnaturally high. "How so?"

"It seems one of the mothers has been gossiping about my son. Why a grown woman would feel the need to take time to talk about a child is beyond me, but there we have it. I just hope I can figure out who it was so I can make sure she doesn't hurt my son's feelings again by speaking more about things she does not understand."

I turned and looked her in the face without a hint of a smile. "Don't you agree?"

Corinne sputtered a bit, then nodded. "Sure, yes. I mean, I do agree."

I let my smile spread slowly. "Wonderful. Maybe we will get very lucky and it won't happen again."

Corinne cleared her throat and turned back to watch the kids. "I'm sure it won't," she said in an extremely small voice.

I relaxed after that, confident that I'd gotten my point across. While Rain was in the dugout, Grizz waved me down with a couple of large sodas. "Thirsty?" he asked.

He was considerate, I'd give him that. "Thanks." I gulped down half of it. "It's hot today." I normally brought cooling towels and a cooler, the whole nine yards. But I'd forgotten today, after waking up so late.

"How's our boy doing?" he asked. "The line was long at the concession stand. I missed him."

I sighed and twisted my lips. "Not so great. He missed a throw that he normally would crack on. I think his uncle has been a bad influence."

Hutch had been over every night this week, keeping Rain laughing and playing. And he'd been up way too late. "We're going to have to keep them from staying up so late," I said. "And maybe push a few veggies and fruits on them."

Rainer headed back out to bat just then, and managed to hit the ball hard enough to make it to first. "Well, at least he squeaked that out," Grizz said. "We'll make sure he gets a bit more rest from now on."

After the game, Rainer didn't feel like going out to pizza with the team. I prayed on the way home it was just the sleepiness and not reluctance to be around people who might judge him for being half bear.

He nearly drifted off on the drive home. When we parked in the garage that I hadn't even seen until our second day there, Grizz sent Rain straight upstairs to shower. "The tiredness is part of his age. We shift for the first time usually between nine and ten."

"Yes," I said as I helped unload all Rain's baseball paraphernalia. "But his birthday isn't for another eight months."

He grabbed the bat bag. "Still, it's normal. From eight to nine, or in the year before the shift. Some kids are earlier or later. But generally, it's about Rain's age."

"A year?" I asked. It seemed like such a long time.

But Rhett shrugged. "It seems like a short time when you think about what a major change he'll go through."

I sighed and stowed Rainer's helmet in the mudroom. "When he does shift, he'll officially be a shifter. But then he can't play. And he loves sports so much."

Rhett took my hand. "I promise, I'll find outlets for our boy. Ones that aren't so strict about shifters."

I nodded, believing him. He would do it.

Rain came downstairs after his shower and was asleep on the couch before Rhett and I even started the grilled cheeses for lunch.

"I'd like to introduce him to some of the shifter kids," Rhett said and handed me the butter. "I think it'd be good for him to be around kids who understand him."

"But won't they judge him from the other side?" I asked. "Look down on his human side?"

Rhett shook his head. "No, I don't think so. That's part of the reason we encourage humans to join our pack and gang. We want people and shifters from all walks of life to feel included in our world. We teach our kids to respect everyone for who they are."

Well, I did like the sound of that, for sure. "Okay," I said. "Okay, then, that sounds nice."

Something occurred to me then. "Wait a minute." I tugged on Rhett's sleeve. "When do I get to see your bear? I never have." The summer I'd spent with him, we'd never gotten around to it, though I'd been dying to. Something about the thought of him shifted, huge and imposing, able to destroy me with one bite, yet knowing he wouldn't... well, that was exhilarating.

Rhett's eyes smoldered as he looked down at me. "Do you really want to see the beast?"

"I do," I whispered. A lot more than I was willing to admit.

"We're having a shifter gathering next weekend. I'll show you then, okay?"

I twisted my lips since I didn't much feel like waiting, but what did I know about shifter life? Maybe he didn't shift all that often. "I suppose I can be patient."

He laughed. "It'll be worth it."

The rest of the weekend passed in a blur of spending time with Rhett and Rainer. Monday dawned and Hutch showed up to go with Grizz and Rain. They were going to the shop, then to meet some other boys around Rainer's age. Two men followed me to Aunt Patty's. As we drove up, two other men got on their bikes and left. Changing of the guards. Well, at least Aunty Patty was safe.

"Morning," I said brightly. Her night nurse had her up and in the recliner. "Hungry?"

"Famished." She grinned at me. "I missed you this weekend, girly."

I rustled up some eggs and laughed at Aunt Patty as I handed her the plate. "What?" I asked. "Why are you staring at me like that?"

"How's it going? Dish!"

I sat on the sofa with my plate and sighed. "It's going wonderfully," I said. "Almost too well."

"What could you mean by that?" She watched me eagerly for the answer.

"Only that I really like him. And things are a lot different, but... still a bit of the same. The good parts are still pretty good. I love that he loves Rain, and he's trying *so* hard to be a good dad."

"And is he succeeding?" she asked.

"Yes," I said, unable to hide my smile. "I think he is. Rainer loves him. He still calls him Grizz, but I'm sure as time goes on, he'll start saying Dad or some variation."

Patty set her plate to the side. "Darling girl." She studied my face for a moment. "Are you sure, absolutely sure that you're ready for this? Raising a shifter?"

I didn't know what to say. "I don't see that I have much of a choice, do I?"

Patty chuckled. "No, but you better prepare yourself now. People have already begun to talk."

"I'm aware," I said dryly. "I don't care about their opinions, or even that they talk, really. As long as Rainer doesn't hear and they treat him well."

"We'll all be on his side," Patty said. "And we'll help."

The rest of the day passed quickly. They usually did with Patty. I did have to do some nursing with her, but really it was like not having a job at all. I didn't look forward to going back to a regular job, not after this fun.

Hutch and I got back to Grizz's house at the same time. Rain ran through the garage and into the house with me and Hutch not far behind. "Was Rhett not with you?" I asked.

Hutch shook his head. "No, he came back early to start dinner, but Big-R and I hung back to finish a job."

I was about to giggle and ask what job, but Rain met us at the door. "Mom, nobody's here."

Hutch's brow furrowed and he pushed past Rain into the mudroom.

"Grizz?" he called. "Hello?"

Suddenly, a sick feeling filled my gut. I held Rainer behind me and inched into the kitchen, but the house was silent.

Hutch appeared across the room, from the direction of the stairs. "I don't think he's here."

Without warning, all the lights in the house went out. Rain threw himself against my back as alarms began to blare, loud ones, like a school having a fire drill.

The worry in my gut turned to terror in an instant.

"Safe room?" I called over the sound of the alarms.

Hutch nodded. "Quickly, go!" He ran behind us with his arms spread, then ended up scooping Rain into his arms. "Faster," he urged.

Thank goodness Grizz had a safe room and thank goodness he'd given me the tour before I unpacked my clothes. The code was hidden behind a panel in his closet. I punched in the numbers and dove in after Rain. Hutch pulled the door closed behind us and we listened to the big, electronic locks engage.

As soon as we were inside the small space and safe, I pulled out my phone. It had no service. "This box is too thick," Hutch explained. He pointed to a phone on the wall. "That one is a separate line that isn't obvious from the outside. If they cut the main phone lines, they'll likely miss this one."

Sure enough, there was a dial tone. "Do you know Grizz's number?" I whispered.

Hutch grimaced and maneuvered his phone out of his pocket to look it up. Even with Rain in his lap, we were cramped in here. At least there was a small vent, and air conditioning pumping into it. Otherwise, we'd swelter before we were rescued.

The only way anyone could get through the air vent would be if they were a mouse shifter... Oh, gosh, was that possible?

But my call went to voicemail. "You don't think...?" I looked at Rain and bit my lip. I didn't want to scare him more, so I kept my freakout internal and to myself.

We sat in silence for another ten minutes before faint beeping interrupted the pressure building in my heart.

"That'll be Grizz," Hutch said. He cocked his head and inhaled deeply. "Yep, Grizz."

How he smelled him from here, I had no idea.

The door opened, and Rhett leaned in and yanked me out, pulling me roughly into his arms. "I was so scared," he whispered. But he didn't hug me long. When Hutch and Rain climbed out, Grizz picked Rain up and gave him just as big of a *bear* hug.

I laughed nervously, my inner joke causing my panic to make me silly. "What happened?" I asked instead of explaining why I was laughing.

Rhett shook his head. "Later."

We went downstairs, and I was as jumpy as a cat at a dog fight, but we went through the motions. Rainer got over it all quickly, but Hutch, Grizz, and I kept exchanging significant glances.

Grizz took Rain to bed as early as he possibly could, spent a good half hour up there, probably reassuring him, then came back downstairs.

"Well?" I asked.

Hutch looked as anxious as I felt. "What was it?" he asked.

"I was coming back from a run when I saw the lights go out. There was someone on the property, but their scent faded at the road. They got in a car. Once I knew they were gone, I came back. All they did was turn off the main breaker. I was able to snap it right back on, though we'll need a new lock for the breaker box."

"Dad always said he was going to move it into the garage," Hutch muttered. "He should've."

"Someone from Chaos was trying another attempt to get me into a war," Grizz said. "The alarm actually scared them off before I even got back. Plus, that alarm deadbolts all doors and locks the windows. The house is pretty damn high tech."

I sighed. "When will this end?" I asked.

Grizz smiled and it looked scary as hell. "I haven't told you the best part. He got in a car, but Reck and a couple of the guys rode up just in time to intercept him. We got the guy."

That didn't make me feel any better.

"We're going to question him and see if we can get this mess over with." Grizz took my hand. "You're safe. Nothing is going to happen to you or Rain."

I let him comfort me. "I know, but that's not what I'm worried about." I met his gaze. "I just got you, and I'm enjoying having you. I don't like the thought of losing you."

Hutch stepped out of the room, then Rhett

pressed a soft kiss to my lips. "I'm not going

anywhere."

Chapter 15 - Grizz

Zoey lay down in bed and seemed to be asleep before she was even completely settled. The fear and adrenaline spike must have taken it all out of her. I was glad since I had business to attend to, and I didn't want her to see what I needed to do.

Leaving her on the bed, I shut the door on my way out. The compound was quiet, with the entire gang either patrolling the exterior, out watching Kim and Aunt Patty's houses, or at the clubhouse, which was on the same property, but a good run away.

My destination was the clubhouse. I reset the house alarm and made sure the door was securely locked before I walked across the yard. Two of my guys were shifted, and their whole job was to circle the house.

The clubhouse was through a copse of trees from the main house, the third point of a triangle between the house and barn. It had a pool table and dart board, a few tables and whatnot. It was a place the gang came to blow off steam or just hang out. There would be no fun there tonight.

I entered and heard the slap of a fist on skin, followed by a gag and cough. I saw Dax wiping blood off his knuckles, with Hutch beside him looking like it was all he could do to hold himself back. A few more of the clan stood behind the prisoner, watching without emotion. Dax turned as I joined the group.

"Little fucker's tough. I may be old, but I've given this shit a good bit of medicine, no info yet," Dax said.

I sneered at the guy in the chair. They'd tied his feet to the legs and his hands to the armrests. His face was covered in fresh cuts and bruises. They'd been working him over pretty good. Hell, his left eye was already swollen shut. The other eye stared at us with a mixture of hate and belligerence. He spat a wad of blood from his mouth right onto my boot. Ugh.

Hutch stepped up with his fangs already elongating. He was ready to shift and eat this guy right then and there.

"Give me a chance, bro, I'll make him talk, I swear I will," Hutch hissed.

I looked at the guy and told Hutch, "Nah, this is my family, my clan, my gang, my home. I am the Alpha. I get to do this."

Hutch stepped back, nodding reluctantly. The guy in the chair smirked at me. He actually fucking smirked at me. He had *no* idea who he was dealing with. I was going to give him one shot to do things the easy way.

I leaned forward, hands on my knees, face inches from his. "Who sent you? *Why* did they send you?"

He looked at me and turned both of his hands, sliding them around under the ropes and flipped me a double bird as an answer. Oh, he thought he was a tough guy.

That was okay. I'd broken tough men before.

Fine, I could play the game both ways.

I went to the dart board and pulled all six darts out, holding them in my fist. The six points all jutted from the bottom of my hand. Without a word, I walked back to him, lifted my fist, and slammed all six points down into the meat of his right quadriceps. He made a sound like a pig being poked with a hot poker, but muffled, since the asshole kept his lips locked together. I left the darts quivering in his leg.

"Do you want more?" I asked.

He bared his teeth at me, the whites tinged with pink from the blood in his mouth. A real tough guy, I'd give him that. I looked at Hutch. "Get that tool bag from the closet."

Hutch hesitated for only a second before sprinting to the coat closet by the door. I didn't think he'd ever seen me like this. Hell, *I'd* never seen me like this. He came back and handed me the red tool bag. The guy on the chair watched the bag cautiously. Sometimes the threat of what I *might* do was enough. I didn't think that would be the case with this dude.

I pulled out a pair of tin snips, super heavy duty scissors, and dropped the bag with a thud. Settling down on one knee in front of him, I looked him dead in the eye. "You come for my woman? You come for my pack? You dared to come to my home and try to lay hands on my boy? *My* boy?" I snapped the tin snips in his face. "You have no idea what you've done."

Lightning quick, I grabbed his right hand, and pulled the middle finger taut, the same finger he just flipped me off with, and put the snips on it.

"Jesus, Grizz," Dax said, his voice worried. I wasn't normally one to take it this far. But he'd crossed the line. His whole gang had.

The man in the chair looked me in the face and said, "You don't got the fucking guts to—"

I didn't let him finish. My hand spasmed closed like a steel band. The snips burst through skin, then muscle, and then the clack of bone breaking in two. And then the finger fell to the floor, the sound of it falling masked by the man's scream. He stared at his hand, sans finger, with bulging eyes. His tough demeanor vanished.

I grabbed his beard with a rough hand and yanked his eyes back to my face, "Names? Plans? Give it to me now! Otherwise?" I slap the tin snips on his crotch, hard, "You know what I cut off next!"

I really hoped I didn't have to do that. No way I wanted to touch this fucker's dick.

The information poured out of him. Everything Brick had heard was correct. It *was* Chaos Crew. The leader, another shifter named Tack, wanted my territory and all that went with it. The relationships with other packs, the money, the respect that came with the Forest Heights name, all of it. The only way to get it was to kill me and all my heirs. He couldn't take over the pack as an Alpha if I, my brothers or any of my kids lived.

Once we were out of the way, Tack could swoop in and claim the territory. He'd kill any of my crew that didn't bow to him as Alpha and then crown himself the new master of Forest Heights.

And definitely, word of my half-human child was out. I should be worried about what would happen when the news made it up the chain to the government, but right now I had a more immediate problem. I could only handle one issue at a time.

I stood up and wiped blood from my hands. The man sat slumped in the chair, sobbing now, fully broken.

Hutch asked, "Do you want us to finish him up? Dump him in the woods somewhere?"

I shook my head. "Nah, I'll be the bigger man. I want this one to send a message back."

I kicked the man in the leg so he lifted his head and looked at me.

"You tell Tack that he has signed his death warrant by fucking with me and mine. You are the warning I'm sending him. And this is the last warning. If he wants a war? It's a war he'll get. And it's a war he will lose."

I had Hutch and Dax load him into a van and dump him in Chaos territory. Before I untied him, though, I made sure to remove the second offending finger. That asshole wouldn't be flipping anyone off ever again.

The rest of that week, I stayed as close to Zoey and Rainer as I could. I really didn't know how desperate or crazy Tack was, but I didn't want to take any chances of them getting hurt. I worked it out so that when Zoey was at work helping her aunt, Rainer came with me to the shop. I spent several days showing him about cars and motorcycles, and even a jet ski someone brought in. It was one of the best weeks of my life. Before I knew it, Friday had come, and it was time for the gathering I'd told Zoey about.

Rainer and I had just picked Zoey up from her aunt's house, and I was driving toward the compound when Rainer spoke. "Hey, Grizz?"

I glanced into the rearview mirror to look at him. "Yeah, bud?"

Rainer bit his lower lip like he was thinking about something really important. "Do you think it would be okay if I called you Pop? Calling you dad just seems a little lame for someone like you."

My hands gripped the steering wheel of the truck so hard I thought I might snap it off the column. A lump formed in my throat, and it was all I could do to keep my emotions from flooding me and pouring out.

I nodded and controlled my voice. "Yeah, man! I would like that. I would actually love that."

He smiled and nodded to himself in the mirror. Zoey wiped tears from her eyes, though she tried to hide it.

"Oh, man, what a bunch of crybabies," I joked.

She laughed and swatted my arm. "Kiss my ass, bear boy. I know you want to cry too. You're just too much of a wannabe badass to admit it."

I chuckled at that, knowing it was pretty true. The rest of the ride, I felt like I was floating, and I had a great feeling about the rest of the night. I pulled into the gravel driveway that led to the compound.

Already, there were tons of people there, easily over a hundred. I hosted a gathering like this once or twice a year, usually on a full moon night. It was every member of the pack and every member of the gang, along with all of their families. These weren't the hedonistic affairs that used to take place up here. These were more family friendly.

Instead of weed and liquor, it was hot dogs and soda, instead of pool and darts, it was volleyball and kickball.

Kim was there already, hanging by the big stack of wood that would turn into a bonfire when the sun went down. Zoey had invited her, and it made me glad. I was happy getting back with me hadn't messed up Zoey's friendship with Kim.

I hopped out of the truck and helped Rainer climb down. Kim saw us and jogged over. She hugged Zoey and ruffled Rainer's hair. "What's up, guys? Ready to party?" Kim asked.

"Yo, bro!" Hutch walked toward us with a girl hanging off him. Must have been his newest chick. She seemed like she was going for a nineties Pamela Anderson vibe. Not much in the way of class.

"Hey, man. I'll find you in a bit, okay?" I said as they walked by.

"Cool!" Hutch waved at Zoey and Rainer, then nodded at Kim, but let his eyes linger on her for a few seconds longer than was normal for a quick hello.

Kim smiled back, and the girl with Hutch looked a little pissed as the two made their way to a group near the barn. Zoey and Kim shared a look that seemed to mean something but *female* was not one of the languages I was fluent in.

I glanced around, trying to find Reck, but he seemed to be missing from the party. I sighed and wished I could get him to get out of his own head. Doc told me the day before that he'd been checking on him, and he was fully healed now, but probably wasn't mentally a hundred percent. I just hoped he'd be back to himself soon.

We had a great time, which made me happy. I wanted Zoey and Rainer to enjoy my inner circle. They were part of it now, and it took a load off my shoulders seeing them enjoy themselves around my second family. Games were played, food was eaten and laughter rang through the compound.

The moon pulled at me, almost making my skin itch with the need to shift. I grabbed a chair and put it in front of the roaring bonfire, then put two fingers in my mouth and whistled. The party quieted as everyone turned to look at me. I had something I needed to say, something they all needed to hear.

"We are The Forest Heights gang! The Forest Heights clan!" I called out after I felt every eye on me. "We are one of the strongest clans in the northwest. We are feared and respected.

There are those who would try to take what we have! There are those who think they deserve what we have just because they want it! I am here to tell you that they deserve nothing! No one *deserves* anything! If you want something, you take it. And, I for one, will destroy anyone who wants to tear apart this family! Will *you* defend this family?"

The crowd screamed in agreement, giving me chills.

"I will die defending you! Will you die defending my family?" I repeated.

The crowd screamed back even louder this time.

"Zo! Come here, please!" I called out. She came but looked hesitant, nervous.

I stepped off the chair and took her hands. "I am so happy to have you back. I want you to know that. I believe, in my heart of hearts, this is where you truly belong. I didn't appreciate what I had all those years ago, but I know now. I will never let you go again. And it's time for you to see the real me."

I stepped away from her and heard the crowd chanting my name, slowly and quietly at first, but getting louder until it turned into a roar as I let my body shift. Fur exploded from my skin, my fingers warped and morphed into clawed paws. A moment later, I stood in front of her, fully changed. Her eyes went wide and shocked.

Finally, she laughed and held a hand out tentatively. "I kind of thought you'd be bigger."

The crowd laughed and I rumbled my own version of bear laughter. She came closer and slid her hand along the fur of my cheek and neck. It felt so good to feel her pet me that way. Warm and welcoming.

"You are an amazing sight to see, Rhett Allen," she said.

I lifted my head and turned my face regally in the firelight, showing off to everyone.

"Oh, don't get all cocky now," she whispered.

My face jolted forward and I slid my tongue from her chin to her hairline.

She squealed and jerked away. "Oh, gross! Do that again, and I'll have a brand new bearskin rug tomorrow!" She pushed at my shoulder. "Just go enjoy your run!"

I lifted myself up onto two legs and roared at the moon. The other shifters in the crowd hooted and screamed as they all began to transform. The humans in the crowd cheered us on as we all sprinted into the forest. As I ran with my pack, taking in the smells and tastes of the forest, I could only think of how lucky I was to have Zoey and Rainer in my life. Later tonight, I'd show her just how grateful I was.

Chapter 16 - Zo

The night passed with a lot of fun; much more than I'd expected. The women attached to the club gathered, mostly humans. The female bears were off running with the pack.

"Hello," a small woman said. "I'm Aliza."

I introduced myself. "I'm Zo. I'm... sort of dating Grizz." What were we? Boyfriend and girlfriend? Shoot, I had no idea.

She laughed. "Sort of. The whole clan has been buzzing with the news of Grizz's human girlfriend and son."

I blushed, thankful that she couldn't see it in the firelight.

"Is this your first run?" Aliza asked as other women gathered, bringing chairs near us and the fire.

I nodded, looking around in surprise as the women began to titter and laugh. "What?" I asked.

"Well, after any run, the guys come back... excited, so to speak," a woman I didn't know said.

Aliza nodded. "But after a clan run, they come back absolutely ravished for us. You'll have to get your son to bed and settled, because Grizz will be *pawing* at you." She winked as we all laughed.

I didn't mind the thought of Grizz all horny. Heaven knew the summer I got pregnant with Rain had been by far the best sex of my life. And it had only been better since I'd come back.

I watched Rain laugh at something one of the other kids said. All the kids not old enough to shift were here, hanging out with their moms. The older ones, around Rain's age, had been disappointed not to go, but it wouldn't be long until he was running behind his father.

What would that feel like, watching my son run off as a bear cub?

Well, I'd cross that bridge when I came to it.

"So, how'd you do it?" an unnamed woman asked.

I looked at her in confusion. "Do what?"

"How'd you get pregnant?" she asked. "Most of us would give our eye teeth to have a baby with these guys. It would be a dream come true."

I shrugged. "I didn't *do* anything except have a wild summer of unprotected sex with Grizz when I was eighteen. I have no idea why or how I got pregnant."

The woman stared at me. "That's it?" she asked in a flat voice.

I pursed one side of my lips. "Sorry. There's no exciting tale. As far as I know, there's only me and one other woman who have gotten pregnant by a shifter. It's probably just an anomaly." I wasn't sure that Grizz wanted the identity of his

other woman and shifter who had a half-shifter

kid revealed, so I didn't mention that he'd told me

about Dax.

"I don't know how, but I'm so thankful for

Rainer," I said. "I can't imagine my life without

him."

"Aren't you worried about the government

interfering?" Aliza asked.

I nodded. "A bit, yeah, but if there's me and

one other I know of, then there must be others.

Surely, they already know it's possible. But maybe

the risk is low enough they don't restrict human

and shifter interaction. Besides, I think half the

women of the world would revolt if they were told

they couldn't sleep with shifters." Everyone laughed and nodded. Several women I knew had at least one fling with a shifter. It was like forbidden fruit and I'd readily admit it was the most delicious of fruits. "All I can do is pray I'm right and that nobody interferes with Rain."

The first of the shifters came out of the forest a while later. And the women were right. They made a beeline for the women and began nuzzling their necks and giving frantic kisses.

Some of them gathered up their children and headed for their cars while others headed off together toward the clubhouse.

I spotted a small group of women, dressed quite provocatively, hanging off to the side. A few of the bears shifted and went straight for those women.

I knew that game. Those were the women who hung around, hoping to be picked up as a girlfriend of the clan. I'd seen motorcycle gang TV shows. It wasn't just a shifter thing.

Grizz was the last one out of the forest.

The kids had gone inside the clubhouse and built a huge fort in the main room. When Grizz came out, he stalked straight for me.

My panties soaked immediately. The look in his eyes was totally predatory, and the sexiest thing I'd ever seen in my life.

He picked me up and at the same time pressed his mouth to mine, sucking on my tongue and growling low in his throat. "Mine," he said, voice gravelly.

I was damn near having an orgasm just from the excitement I knew was coming. "Okay," I whispered. "Yours. But let me walk past Rain."

He growled again and set me on my feet at the door to the clubhouse. We headed in, and I peeked in the fort with my core on fire, praying Rain wouldn't need anything so I could go do what Grizz so desperately wanted to.

To my surprise, the kids were all in a big pallet, sound asleep. I pulled my head out and pressed my finger to my lips. "They're out like little lights."

Grizz grinned and pulled me into his arms again. "Good."

He carried me like that, like a newlywed, up the stairs and into his bedroom.

As soon as the door closed behind us, he set me down, his hands instantly flying to the hem of my shirt.

"It looks exactly the same," I said, looking around the room as he pulled my shirt over my head. "The room I lost my virginity in."

Grizz paused with his hands on my bra clasp. "This time, I won't be so gentle."

Oh, boy, I sure hoped not.

"I'm going to fuck you like you belong to me. Because I damn sure belong to you." His words seared a place in my heart. When had we gotten this serious?

And when had I gotten so okay with it?

Whenever it was, I turned and let my bra slide down my arms. Sometime while he'd taken my shirt and bra off, he'd completely stripped himself. "In a hurry?" I asked.

Looking down, I knew the answer to my question. Rhett's dick pointed straight at me, and when my gaze hit it, he made it bounce.

"I'm in a hurry to feel you clench around me, yes," he replied.

I unbuttoned my jeans and kicked off my shoes as I backed toward the bed and he stalked me. "Take what you want, then," I whispered.

Grizz pounced, lifting me up and both of us landed on the bed. In another second, he had my jeans and panties pulled off as his mouth found my nipple, sucking hard and eagerly. "Rhett," I whispered.

He didn't wait. Lifting up long enough to reach into the bedside drawer, he pulled out a condom, slid it on, then sank himself deeply inside me with a sigh that told me he'd been dying to do it. "Fucking hell, Zo. It's like coming home."

"Move," I urged him, and he complied, thrusting his hips in and out, then reaching one hand between us to press against my clit.

"I want to hear your moans," he said in my ear as he filled me over and over.

It was easy to give him what he wanted. I let my mouth fall open and whatever sounds wanted to escape me had free rein as I gripped his shoulders.

"Damn it," he muttered. "Please let me take this condom off. I want to feel you, your skin, your moisture around me. If you get pregnant, I'll do it right this time, I swear."

I swallowed and made myself focus. "I don't think I'm at the right time to ovulate," I said. Fuck, why not? "Okay."

He pulled out and took off the condom, then when he slid inside me again, it really did feel better. I cried out as he began to move, faster and harder. After a few minutes, an orgasm built, partly from his thrusts as his head slammed into my G-spot, and partly from his finger on my clit. It exploded over me and I yelled his name from deep in my throat as my walls clenched, milking him.

He pulled out and flipped me over, moving me like it was no big deal, like I was light as a feather.

I settled down on my elbows and bit back a scream of pleasure as he slipped into me again. "God, you're creamy," he said as the sounds of his pelvis slapping into mine filled the air.

That noise turned me on even more. I rocked back into him, his cock filling me deeper and deeper every time. "More," I urged. "Harder!"

"I don't want to hurt you." He was holding back.

"I'll tell you if it hurts," I gasped out. "Give me more!"

I moved my arms down so my chest sank into the bed, then screamed into the mattress when he did as I'd asked and started hitting harder and faster.

"I won't last long this way," he said. His voice was growling again, deep. It rumbled through me like a vibrator on my clit.

I turned my face out of the mattress so I could speak. "I'm coming now," I said, then reached down to rub my clit, enhancing the orgasm that had just begun.

His thrusts lost control, turning frantic, and it did nearly hurt then, but not quite.

And then he slowed to a stop, panting. The timing couldn't have been better as my orgasm waned, slowly fading away.

Grizz collapsed beside me and gathered me in his arms. "Did I hurt you?" he asked.

I twisted around so I could look up at him and still be held. "No," I whispered. "It was perfect."

"Wow." He winked at me. "I didn't hold back at the end."

"Then I can take you at your hardest," I said. "And I really liked it."

He chuckled and held me closer. "I'm so glad you're back in my life."

"Me, too," I said, pulling away so we could look at each other. "I really am."

"I promise I'm going to do right by you this time," he said. He seemed a little nervous.

"What is it?" I asked.

"I want to claim you." His voice went soft. "I want you to be my mate."

That sounded like... like it was what I'd been meant to do all my life. Except, I didn't fully know what it meant. "What does that entail?" I asked, now feeling a bit nervous myself.

"Well, I've never heard of a shifter taking a human mate," he said. "But it's not gory or anything. I bite you, and my fangs go into your skin and my saliva is injected. Biting is a thing with bears, and if we'd kept on after that summer, I would've probably bitten you. But the mating bite is a lot more significant."

I nodded. "That's something we can seriously think about," I said.

"When you're ready." Rhett pressed a kiss to my temple. "I won't go faster than you're comfortable with."

Sleep started to wear at me. It'd been a long day. "I'm glad Rain seems to be fitting in," I said after a big yawn.

"He's the alpha's son. Of course he's fitting in."

I laughed and cuddled closer. "Is it as easy as that?" I asked.

"Easy as that."

It would be good for him. At least I didn't have to worry about him being lonely or rejected like with the baseball team. Maybe I'd think about pulling him off the team earlier than his first shift. Whatever was best for my boy.

That was my last thought, and I slept like a rock, which was fairly unusual for me.

Multiple orgasms were pretty powerful sleep aids.

When I woke the next morning, my stomach growled at me. Rhett was snoring away, so I got up and put my clothes back on. I knew where the clubhouse kitchen was, and if nobody had started breakfast, I would. Rain would be hungry, too, and I didn't want him to wake up and go looking for us in a clubhouse full of people who had done the nasty all night.

I crept down the hall, but a voice on the phone caught my attention. I peeked in the crack of the door to see Reck on his cell. I started to go in and ask if he'd like some breakfast, but then his conversation sank in. He said something about meeting up and when he said Grizz didn't know about it, I backed up to listen in the shadows of the hallway where he couldn't hear me.

"I've got things handled," he said quietly. "Nobody suspects anything. Don't worry."

This conversation gave me a very bad

feeling, but I wasn't going to confront a bear

about it. Reck was in a bad place, according to

Grizz. I'd tell him about it as soon as I could. With

Reck's history, this couldn't be anything good.

Chapter 17 - Grizz

I was coming down the hall to look for Rainer to see if he wanted to play catch outside when I heard Reck. He was cursing under his breath about there not being any beer in the fridge. I stopped in the hallway, listening to him close the refrigerator door, and tried to think of what to say to him. We'd all given him a lot of space the last few weeks, but he'd still been in this weird sullen, depressed mood. Sneaking in and out of the compound at the weirdest damn hours. To be honest I was losing my patience and getting pissed at him.

I stepped forward to speak, but froze when I heard a voice call out to him first. It was Rainer.

"Hey, Reck!"

"Oh, hey, buddy. What's up?" Reck replied. I leaned back so they wouldn't see or hear me.

"Nothin'. Hey, so why do you hide out in your room all the time?"

Shit, I needed to stop this. Only kids would ask questions like that. But Reck was already talking, so I stayed still.

"Well, my man, there's a lot of bad people in this world. Those people like to hurt other people. I was one of the ones who got hurt. So I decided to just stay inside and let the bad people have the rest of the world."

Rainer replied, "Were they bullies?"

Reck chuckled. "Yeah, basically, they were bullies."

"Mom told me once that bullies only do what they do because they're just jealous. Maybe your bullies are jealous of you?"

Reck burst out laughing, the deep infectious laugh that I hadn't heard in a couple of months. I'd forgotten how much I'd missed it until right then.

Reck asked, "Hey, have they given you a club name yet, big guy?"

Rainer huffed a breath and said, "They all just call me runt because I'm little." Compared to humans, he was a big kid. But compared to other shifter boys his age, he was fairly small. Not that much, though.

I had to bite the knuckle of my hand to keep from laughing. Everyone knew the kid was itching to get a real club name so he could feel like he was one of the guys, a real member. Names weren't given out until they were patched into the club. Patching in was like a mini ceremony, they got the symbol of the club tattooed on their bodies, and then they got the same symbol patch sewn onto their jacket. There were still quite a few years until Rainer would be old enough to patch into Forest Heights. Though, maybe with him being my first and only son we might make an exception.

Reck whistled quietly. "Well, we can't have that now, can we? Hmm, I've got it!"

"What? What is it?" Rainer asked.

"I'm gonna call you Lil' Grizz, since you're so much like your dad."

Rainer's voice dropped to a whisper, and even I could barely hear him, "Do you really think I'm like my Pop?"

There was silence for a few seconds, then Reck cleared his throat. When he spoke, he sounded a little choked up. "Yeah, bud. I really do."

I turned around and left them there, walking quietly so they didn't hear me. It made me happy that my boy was maybe helping my brother get out of the dark place he'd been for so long. God knew Reck needed to get out of his funk.

I found Zoey in the kitchen. I was going to grab her ass, but saw the look on her face and knew something was wrong.

"What is it?" I asked.

She glanced at me and bit her lower lip. She looked like she was having an argument inside her own head. Whatever was bothering her, it was something she didn't *really* want to say out loud. She turned around and leaned on the counter, folding her arms across her chest.

"I heard something a little while ago. It made me kind of uncomfortable."

I frowned, confused. "What was it?"

"I overheard Reck on the phone with someone. He didn't know I was around. It sounded like he was planning or plotting something. Whatever it was, it didn't sound good. I haven't felt right since I heard it."

I stared at her for a minute before shaking my head. "No, I think you must have heard wrong. Reck's been through a lot of shit lately. There's no way he'd be planning something, especially nothing that might get him in trouble."

She pursed her lips and leaned into me. "No, Grizz, I didn't *hear wrong*! I'm telling you he's planning...I don't know. Like I said, I only heard his side, but he was talking about how you weren't suspicious and that none of us knew anything."

I didn't want to argue, but I was getting a little pissed that she would accuse my brother of something like that. "Listen, Zo, I know you think you heard something, but I don't really take kindly to you basically calling Reck a snake in the grass. We call him Reck because he's reckless. He's not a snake."

Her jaw dropped. "I didn't call him a snake. Okay? You can believe me or not, but I don't want Rainer alone with him."

I ground my teeth together. "Now, wait a minute! You are not going to stand here and say my brother would hurt my son are you?"

She rolled her eyes at me. "Now you're just putting words in my mouth. I never said that. But, there are bad people after us. They tried to kill Reck once before just to piss you off. Who says it might not happen again? If Rainer is with Reck when that happens, then what do you think the outcome might be? All because of some stupid-ass turf war?"

"That's just horseshit. Reck knows to stay safe now. He'd never put Rainer in danger."

Zoey grabbed her keys and lifted a hand for me to stop. "We can talk about this later, I have to go to work." She turned and called down the hall. "Rainer! I'm going to Aunt Patty's."

Rainer came bounding down the hall and gave her a hug. Zoey kissed the boy on the head and turned to leave, but she didn't even look back at me on the way out the door. I watched her walk out to the car and drive away.

Her words echoed in my head, but I dismissed them again. My brother was a hothead, and he could be stupid, but he was loyal. He would never betray anyone he loved, never. I couldn't believe Zoey would even try to bring up something like that.

I ruffled Rainer's head. "I got to go to the shop really quick. You hang here with your Uncle Reck. I'll be back in an hour or so. Okay?" I'd be damned if I'd let Zoey dictate that my brother couldn't watch my son.

"Yeah, sure." Rainer grabbed a plate and piled eggs high. He seemed content to stay here.

The shop was open, but I needed to stop in and check on things. I hadn't spent much time there since finding out about Chaos being after me, and there were some things I needed to do before the end of the week. I hopped on my bike and let the wind wipe the argument with Zoey out of my head. I got to the garage about twenty minutes later. I had barely gotten into the office when my phone rang. It was Hutch.

"What's up?" I asked.

"Got a problem. Brick called, and said there's been a sighting of some Chaos boys in town."

My anger surged along with the nagging ache of fear. "How many?"

"Didn't say, but it sounds like a pretty decent sized crew."

"Dammit! Okay, Rainer is at the compound with Reck. You get over there too, just so there's some backup if they try something. I'll meet you there soon. Make sure the boys all have eyes on Zo, got it?"

"On it, big bro." He hung up.

I jogged out without even speaking to the shop team. I jumped back on my bike and kicked the engine to life, leaving a strip of rubber in the

parking lot as I pulled out.

At that moment, I didn't care about getting

pulled over. I pushed the bike up to nearly ninety,

even getting over a hundred on some of the

straightaways. I was back at the compound

driveway in less than fifteen minutes. Hutch's bike

was already there, so he was inside with Rainer

and Reck. I stopped outside the barn and finally

pulled out my phone to call Zoey. Things here

looked fine, and she needed to know to keep an

eye out.

It rang twice before she answered, "Yes?"

She still sounded pissed.

"Hey, I know you're mad, but I need you to keep your head on a swivel, okay?"

Her voice went from cold detachment to worry in an instant. "What's happened?"

"One of the boys called and said a bunch of Chaos guys are moving around town. I have guys watching you and everyone else, you just need to be safe and stay alert."

"What about Rainer? Is he still safe?"

I nodded as if she could see me. "He's good. Hutch is with him, I—"

A bloodcurdling bear roar cut through the morning air. I almost dropped the phone, then. It wasn't Hutch's roar, it was Reck.

"Zo, I gotta call you back!" I hung up and threw the phone on the ground.

I sprinted to the compound. Another roar came from the backyard of the house. My boots spat gravel up as I ran. I moved faster than I've ever gone in my life. I rounded the corner and saw Reck, in bear form, lying on his side.

A deep gash ran down his right arm, blood seeping from it into the dirt. He was pawing at the air, staring into the woods behind the compound. I slid to a stop and looked toward the back door. Hutch, in human form, lay across the threshold. He was unconscious, blood smeared across his face. My stomach dropped, and I almost vomited right then. The fear and confusion was almost enough to bring up my breakfast.

I stepped over to Reck as he shifted back to human form, pale and sickly. He finally turned away from the woods and looked into my eyes and said the thing I knew he was going to say.

"They took him! They took him, man! I'm so fucking sorry, Grizz."

I yelled into his face. "What do you mean they took him? Who?"

Reck pushed himself into a sitting position and cradled his injured arm, the cut already slowly stitching itself back together. He looked nervous and ashamed. Whatever he was going to say, I knew I wasn't going to like it.

I let my face shift, and roared into his face, spittle flying into his eyes, the wind from my voice made his hair flutter.

My face went human again. "SPEAK!"

He sobbed as he talked. "Beating me up wasn't just to piss you off and take your territory. I...I'd felt so out of place in the pack, the gang. I was the youngest, right? I was never going to be Alpha. I was just, like, in the background. Everyone just thinking I was fucking Reck! A reckless kid, not good for a damn thing. I felt worthless, so I started hanging with some Chaos guys a few months back. They made me feel like less of a burden, like I was someone."

Tears rolled down his cheeks as betrayal and fury grew in my gut. "I thought they were my friends, so I started telling them stuff. But they were using me, man. They wanted me to betray you. When I refused, that was when they almost killed me. To make an example of me."

My hands clenched into fists, getting tighter as he spoke. I did not like where this was going. I needed to go check on Hutch, but I had to hear this story to the end.

Reck swiped snot away from his nose with his sleeve. "They called earlier today and said they needed me to do something, and this time if I didn't follow through, they'd really kill me. So I just listened to what they wanted, and played along."

Fuck me. Zoey had been right. She'd been right the whole damn time!

"I didn't really agree, I never would! They wanted me to bring Rainer to them at seven tonight. I was actually getting ready to bring Rainer to the shop to see you. To tell you everything. But Hutch pulled up, and before I could explain any fucking thing, the Chaos boys jumped us. They came out of the woods, took down Hutch before he could shift. I did what I could, but...fuck, bro—"

I grabbed him by the throat before he could finish. "Don't! Don't you fucking call me brother!

Not when you let them take my son! A real brother would have died first!" I pointed at Hutch's unconscious body. "That is a real brother! A man! You are a fucking child! You are going to tell me everything about Chaos, their members, their compound, everything! And you'll help me get my boy back! If there is so much as a scratch on Rainer…"

Reck was sobbing now. His heart was broken by the way I was talking to him, but right then, I didn't care. Hutch groaned behind me, giving me a slight relief that he was still alive, but not enough to dampen my anger. "If they so much as touch a hair on his head, you'd better be prepared for the consequences."

I shoved him away from me to cry in the

dirt. I lifted my face to the sky, and let out a roar

unlike any I'd ever made. It exploded from my

throat, and echoed for minutes afterward.

Chapter 18 - Zo

The bad feeling wouldn't shake. No matter what I did, it stuck with me. But it was the first argument I'd had with Grizz since we'd started seeing each other again, and it was like a mimic of when he hadn't believed I was pregnant. If Rhett Allen didn't respect me enough to trust that I wouldn't lie to him, about pregnancies or overhearing conversations, then I didn't know what I was doing, kicking things up with him again.

I couldn't sit still, and Aunt Patty was taking a nap, so I started cleaning. Something was wrong, and I kept thinking maybe it was something bigger than just the argument, but then I brushed it off as me being paranoid.

Then again, Reck had been planning something. What could it have been? I stewed on it as I changed all the sheets in the house and started a load of laundry.

"Zo?" Aunt Patty called.

I darted into her room. "Hey, I didn't know you were up," I said as I helped her sit up and get in her chair.

"I've been awake for a good twenty minutes," she said. "Watching you dart back and forth, cleaning this room then that one. What's going on? Where's your head at?"

I sat on the other side of her bed and sighed, then told her the whole story of what happened between me and Grizz.

When I was finished, Aunty Patty sighed. "Well. That's quite a conundrum. It can't be easy for someone in Grizz's position to believe that someone he loves and cares about is trying to betray him or is up to no good. Especially when the person is his brother."

I glared at her. "Please don't come at me with reason and rational thoughts."

Patty chuckled and reached over to pat my arm. "Honey, that's what I'm here for. And I also think it's perfectly normal that you'd be upset that he didn't believe you. Especially after he didn't believe you were pregnant with his baby." She reached over for a sip of her water. "Can you get me some more?"

"Of course!" I jumped up and circled the bed to get her bottle.

"You did right by telling him." She handed me the refillable bottle with a funny saying on the side. "Even though it seems like it blew up in his face right now."

I felt a lot better after our talk. I had been contemplating if saying anything had been a good idea to begin with. After I got Aunt Patty settled in the living room, I grabbed the cleaning caddy and headed upstairs to the bathroom the night nurse used. She made minimum wage and wasn't a full-blown nurse, but she only had to do something if Patty woke in the night, so it was a pretty sweet gig. She had a day job she did on top of the nights, so she was happy to be here.

The bathroom didn't look like it needed to be cleaned, but I needed something to do and I'd already gone over the kitchen and downstairs bathroom. I gave it a good scrubbing from the shower to the toilet, to the vanity, then headed back down with pruny fingers, thinking about getting some lotion from Patty. I should've worn gloves. Those cleaners were harsh. I stowed the caddy under the kitchen sink, then my phone lit up from the kitchen table. Oh, shoot, I'd left it turned down.

I picked it up and tapped the screen to find fifteen missed calls and thirteen texts. As I unlocked the phone, someone banged on the front door, hard.

Rushing through the living room, I tried to tap the icon for my messages, but my finger missed. Instead of trying again, I looked through the peephole.

"Let me in!" Hutch yelled as I spotted him.

I undid the locks and let him in. "What is going on?" He walked in looking incredibly rough. He was pale, almost deathly so, and blood was spattered all over his clothes. "Are you okay?"

Hutch looked into my eyes, and guilt was written all over his face. "I tried to fight them off," he said in probably the most miserable voice I'd ever heard.

My stomach clenched in terror. "Where is my son?" I whispered. But I already knew.

"Rainer was taken," Hutch said in a quiet voice.

My knees nearly buckled. Hutch grabbed my arm, but I didn't need him. I couldn't fall apart.

"Where is he?" Patty asked. I'd forgotten she was sitting in her electric chair in front of the TV.

Hutch started talking, but his words didn't make any sense to me. I walked into the kitchen and dialed the number for the night nurse. "Hey,

Connie. I've got a family emergency. Can you come in early?" I asked.

"Sure," she said. "The timing is good, I can come now."

After thanking her profusely, I grabbed my keys and went back to the living room. "You okay until Connie gets here?" I asked Patty. "Grizz's guys are outside, but they're not nurses."

She waved me off. "Of course! But please, fill me in the moment you know something."

"I will."

Hutch already had the front door open, waiting on me to come through.

"Love you, Patty," I called as I ran out.

Hutch had Grizz's truck. I darted to the passenger seat and jumped in. "Now, tell me what happened."

"We were hanging out and some of the Chaos boys came out of nowhere," he said miserably. "I tried to fight them off, but they nearly killed me. I'm still damn weak."

"Didn't Reck take a long time to heal when he was injured severely?" I asked with blood pounding in my ears.

"Yeah," he said. "I'll be okay, just weak for a while."

I wanted to kill him myself for letting my boy be taken.

He drove us straight to the compound, then to the clubhouse. As soon as I jumped out of the truck, I ran for the door, and Hutch barely was able to get ahead of me, clutching his side.

I followed him to a door I'd never been through. "Grizz is holding church," Hutch said with his hand on the doorknob.

"I don't care if he's got God himself in there," I hissed. "Move."

Hutch shrugged and opened the door. The entire club looked like they were inside. The room was big, but it looked small because of all the bodies in there. What I assumed were the core members of the club sat around a large wooden table with Grizz at the head. An empty chair to his right must've been for Hutch. On the other side of that chair was Reck.

He opened his mouth, but I held up one hand, fury floating through me like a black smoke. "If anything happens to my son, you won't have to worry about Chaos coming after you. I will take you out myself."

"Zoey," Grizz said, but I turned my glare on him.

"And you. If you'd listened, my baby wouldn't be out there in the hands of people who hate him. If anything happens to him, I swear, I'll never forgive you."

He stood. "If anything happens to our son, I'll never forgive myself."

Grizz gestured toward the empty chair beside him. I sat begrudgingly, and Hutch perched on the table behind Grizz, but I turned and glared at Reck until he jumped up. "Sit here, Hutch."

Once we were settled, Reck started speaking. "I've drawn out their compound," he said. "I've been to it a couple of times. I don't know all the rooms, but this is the basic layout." It looked like they had two buildings. "This is a garage, and this is their clubhouse. Everyone in the club lives there. They're not allowed to live offsite."

"That sounds ridiculous," Dax said.

"It is," Reck said. "But if I had to guess, they'll have Rain in their church room, too." He pointed to a room in the back of the clubhouse. "But they could have him in any of the bedrooms."

"Did they tell you what they'd do with him?" Grizz asked through clenched teeth.

Reck shook his head. "No, and I never intended to let it get to an actual kidnapping. I was coming to tell you when they showed up here. I guess they knew I wouldn't be able to go through with it and double-crossed me."

Anger, fear, revulsion. I couldn't pinpoint all the emotions washing through me as I watched and listened to the club plan how they could go get Rainer.

Grizz's phone rang as they were working on how to approach the building as one unit from all sides.

Grizz put it on the table and pressed the button to answer, then put it on speaker.

"This is Tack," a man said in a gruff voice. "I've got something that belongs to you."

"Mom?" Rainer's voice ran all through me, bringing tears to my eyes. Then he screamed as if they were hurting him, and my heart shattered.

I opened my mouth to yell at the man to let him go, but Hutch pulled me into his arms and clamped his hand over my mouth. "No," he whispered.

Hutch's arms stayed tightly around me as I watched Grizz. I hated him in that moment, him and Reck and the whole club. I glared at the lot of them.

"Meet me. My clubhouse," Tack said. "And when I take you out and take your place as alpha of the Hangmen, then I'll give your son to his mother."

"We're on our way," Grizz said.

"Alone," Tack growled. "Or he dies."

"Fine." Grizz's fists opened and closed on the table. "I'll come alone." He hung up and Hutch let me go.

"I hope those screams haunt you twice as much as they will me," I hissed.

Reck, standing behind Grizz, grimaced and tears slipped down his cheeks.

"Let's go get my son," Grizz said, standing. "We'll use Dax's formation to get on the property."

He stared solemnly at his crew. "Take out anyone who gets in the way. Don't take them down. Take them out. Tack is mine. I'm not giving him my territory and I'm not giving him my son."

He looked at me then. "Stay at my house. Please."

"Will I be safe there?" I asked. "Rain wasn't safe here."

He barely flinched, but I saw the direct hit my words had been in his eyes.

"I fucked up," he said in a quiet voice. "I don't blame you for not trusting me, but I love you, Zoey. I love you so fucking much, and I won't survive something happening to you and Rainer. I'll get our boy back, but I can't focus if I'm worried about your safety, too." He paused for a second as my nostrils flared. "Will you please stay there? Will you go stay in my safe room?"

I barely managed to keep the tears at bay. "Fine," I spat out. "I'll stay. But you better bring my boy home."

"I will," he said. "I promise."

Chapter 19 - Grizz

The boys were getting ready. I'd never seen them like this. Every one of them buzzed with adrenaline. So did I, but I had to talk to Zoey before we went. She'd gone off to the house after church was over. I made my way over, dreading how this would go.

I found her in our room, pacing back and forth. Her head snapped toward me as I entered; her eyes looked like they were trying to bore through me.

Before she could speak, I held up my hands. "I'm sorry, okay? I just had a hard time believing

Reck would do something like this. I never, in a million years, thought he would betray us. I should have never treated you like you were lying. I'm an asshole, and I'm sorry."

"No, I get it. I do, I get why you didn't believe me, but look at the situation you put us in. I'm fucking pissed! But we are a team, and don't forget that I'm a part of your family now. Just like Hutch, just like Reck." She sucked in a deep breath. "As angry as I am, my son is still a shifter. I still need him to be here. And damn it all, I still care about you and even Hutch. And Reck, when it comes down to it."

I nodded, not saying anything. I just walked to her and took her in my arms. She was stiff and hesitant at first, but relaxed after a moment. I gave her a gentle kiss, and was grateful she kissed me back.

Pulling away, I looked into her eyes. "I promise that I will make this up to you. I don't know how, but I will. Once I get our boy back, I will make it up to both of you. I love you. I love you so much."

She stared back at me and hesitated. Her chest heaved as I prayed to anyone who would listen that she'd give me a chance to prove to her that it wouldn't always be like this.

She warred with herself internally, though it was written all over her face for several seconds before she finally said, "I love you too."

***

It was almost one in the morning before my crew got within striking distance of the Chaos compound. I was kneeling in the grass on the edge of the woods encircling their setup, which was bigger than our own, and they only had a main building and a garage. Hutch was next to me, my second-in-command. I'd tried to get him to stay behind but he wouldn't have it.

I looked at him. "We split up. You take half the crew, I'll take the other. Just in case Reck didn't know what the hell he was talking about, and Rainer is in a different spot. Leave two guys out in the woods. If somehow Tack runs, with or without Rainer, they can track him."

"Sounds good, bro. Hey." He raised a fist toward me. "Till Valhalla?"

"We aren't in the military, man."

"No. But it's cool as shit to say, though."

I grinned and tapped my fist against his anyway. I turned and lifted a hand to the crew. We were fifty strong with more than half of us shifters, their eyes were like glittering gems in the darkness. They were waiting for my signal. These men were ready to fight and die for my boy, for me. I dropped my hand, slicing through the air toward the compound.

The signal given, the crew sprinted out of the forest toward the main building. We moved like ghosts, half the gang splitting and following Hutch to the back side of the massive building, the rest following me. A sentry stepped out from behind the garage. Dax leaped, shifting in midair and fell upon him before he could scream.

My team was at the door before the first halogen spotlights burst into light. I slammed my massive shoulder into the door, satisfied when it burst off of its hinges, and fell to the ground. There were so many Chaos crew members inside, it actually stunned me for a split second. More than I'd anticipated, for sure, at least twenty in this room alone. The seconds seemed to slow, almost like time had stopped. I watched, with superhuman clarity, Chaos crew members standing, shifting, grabbing guns. Then, like a light switch was tripped, everything sped into hyper-speed.

I shifted and dove into battle. Gunshots, screams, and roars slammed against my ears. I crashed into two humans, swiping at them with my claws. They both fell screaming, dropping their guns. I locked my jaws onto the throat of a Chaos shifter and tasted his fur on my tongue as I drove him into the wall, knocking him unconscious. The hornet buzz of a bullet whipped past my ear. Turning, I watched Brick bring a chair down on top of the man who took the shot at me. We had the element of surprise, and my gang took the room easily. It felt like days, but couldn't have been more than two minutes of fighting. The Chaos members were either unconscious, dead or surrendering to my boys.

I was going to go mad. Where the hell was my boy?

A woman's scream behind me nearly made me jump. I looked and watched one of my guys pulling two Chaos chicks out from behind a big couch at the back of the room. They brought them to me.

"Look at me!" I shouted at them at the top of my voice.

They stopped screaming and looked at me with fearful eyes.

Lowering my voice, I growled. "A little boy, looks just like me. Where the fuck is he? I swear to god, you better not lie to me."

The blonde glanced at the bar that stood on the left wall. I watched her eyes move, and turned to look. All I could see was a rack of liquor and wine. I turned back to her.

"Don't say anything," the brunette whispered to the blonde.

I clutched her chin in my hand and growled in her face.

The blonde sobbed, then blurted, "I saw them take a kid through the hidden door. Over there. Pull the bottle of vodka on the bottom shelf."

I pushed her away and motioned for the boys to follow me. Gunshots and roars came from a different part of the compound, but I couldn't let myself worry about Hutch or my other guys. I was laser-focused on my boy. Rainer and nothing else.

Brick pulled the vodka bottle. It was actually a lever. There was a click and the whole wall moved back two inches. I took a half-dozen guys through the door with me, leaving the rest to guard our backs. We got down three flights of stairs before we found more Chaos members. This time they knew we were coming, but there were only three of them.

They came at us from a hallway to the right. Jesus, how big was this place? I worried about my son as we fought our way through them. They knew we were here, so what might they do to him?

Leaving two men unconscious and the third screaming, holding his hand that was now missing three fingers, bitten off by one of my shifters, we went down the same hallway Chaos had come from. It ended in a doorway.

My hands shook harder. Each second that went by without finding Rainer drove me further into a combination of berserker rage and panic.

One of my team kicked the door down, and we flooded in. I slid to a halt, my chest tightened, a sigh of breath leaked from my lips. Rainer was alive and tied to a chair. I pushed my men aside and got closer. He had a cut above his eye, and the other eye was swollen. They'd hit him. They'd struck my boy. A red film slid over my vision, and my body nearly vibrated with rage. Anger unlike any I'd ever experienced had me in its grip. I almost spontaneously shifted, would have, had the voice of Tack not startled me out of my haze.

"You stay right there, big'un!" Tack called.

I looked at the man. He was shirtless, his torso crisscrossed with scars of past fights. He stepped forward and I took note of his bulging knuckles and his boulderlike shoulders. He was smaller than me, but was in incredible shape. I knew in an instant that he was a fighter.

"Now, me and you got some business, don't we?" Tack said smiling. He didn't seem to care that I had six more shifters with me and that he was only him.

"You'll die for touching my boy. Do you hear me?" I growled. It was all I could do not to look at my son. Every time I did, he stared back at me with huge eyes. I didn't dare untie him yet. He might try to interfere and get even more hurt than he already was.

He smiled and nodded. "Yup, yup, that *is* what I thought you'd say. That will be settled soon enough. In the here and now, though? I challenge you for the title of Alpha of Forest Heights clan. I challenge, and only a coward declines that. You lose, I cut that thick throat of yours, then I plug ya' boy full of holes and let him bleed out. You win? Well, I'll be honest...ain't gonna happen. Whatcha' gonna say, Big Grizz?"

I glanced at my men. They knew what a challenge like that meant. They nodded and stepped back. I was on my own. If I lost, Tack would be within his rights to kill Rainer and take control of my clan, my whole gang. I grinned at him humorlessly. "I never lose. I accept." This wasn't my first challenge, and likely wouldn't be my last. I glanced one time at my son to see tears rolling down his cheeks as he struggled against his bonds.

I had to put him out of my mind and focus on the fight because without another word, Tack leapt forward, closing the ten feet between us in two steps, shifting before I knew what was happening. I'd never seen anyone move so fast.

He slammed into me and drove me to the ground. I put my hands up, clutching his chest as his teeth clacked together, inches from my throat. His drool dripped into my face and neck. He was so damn strong, and I couldn't shift until I got some room between us. I started kicking and kneeing at his balls, finally making contact. He tensed and rolled off me just long enough for me to push myself away, using the moment to shift.

Tack was a huge black bear, but I was a grizzly. Black bears had nothing on us.

I roared and charged him. He swatted at me, catching me in the snout, but I didn't hesitate. I hit him dead in the chest and knocked him back nearly ten feet. I heard a rib snap when I made contact. Rearing up on two feet, I let my weight fall down onto him, slamming my paws into his face as I came down. Blood exploded from the black nostrils of his face. I watched his eyes roll in his head. He nearly went unconscious then.

But before I could attack again, his paw shot out and swept my leg from under me. I tumbled heavily to my side and he was back on top of me. He bit me deeply in the shoulder, blood squirted from the wound. Instead of screaming, I bit at the side of his head. My jaws clamped on his right ear, I jerked my head to the side with such force the ear tore away.

Tack rolled away, howling, and shifted back to his human form. He kept rolling on the floor screaming and clutching at his missing ear. Blood poured from between his fingers. I shifted back to my human skin too and stepped over to him, blood still flowing from my bitten shoulder.

"It's done! I win. Now, I will show you mercy if you get the fuck out of here. Leave my pack, my territory, and my family alone. I'll give you two days to get as far away from here as you can. Out of Idaho, out of the west! Hell, you'd better get as far east as you can and you better not even step foot across the Mississippi after that. Got it?" I said.

Tack got himself under control and sat up on his knees, gasping in pain. "All right, big dude. No hard feelings, right? Ain't no need for two bears to go out like this."

Tack's left hand snapped up, already shifting, and before I could move, his claws raked the side of my face. Blood flew from my cheek as I fell backward, shifting, and the fight became a whirlwind. Our claws and teeth ripped and tore at each other. It went on for what felt like days.

Finally, exhausted, I tried to roll away to catch my breath, but Tack bit my right arm and shook his head violently, trying to rip it off. He was so strong, I was sure the limb would come out any second. I roared, my rage supplanting my pain and exhaustion, the fury of what he'd done to my son giving me a last bit of energy.

I jerked my head forward, latching onto Tack's throat and biting down hard, hearing skin and muscle start to crackle under my jaws. I yanked my head back, hard, harder than I'd ever pulled in my life. His throat came out as I tugged. Blood poured out of him as I crawled away, and the black bear squealed and spasmed on the ground for a few seconds before going still, his black eyes staring, vacant, at the ceiling.

I spat out the wad of flesh and fur and then shifted back to human. I sat for several seconds, gasping for breath, feeling the thousand aches and pains across my body, my ears ringing. Where was my son? Whirling, panting and exhausted, I met his gaze. He'd stopped crying, but his chest still heaved as Tack's men rushed past me to their dying leader's side.

This was going to be one hell of a mess. If I'd challenged Tack in return, I would now be the Alpha of Chaos as well as Forest Heights, but I hadn't, so their clan would need to vote on a new Alpha.

I didn't give a shit about all that, that was something they would need to figure out. But several shifters had died tonight. I would need to file the case with the government. I'd need affidavits from witnesses, I'd have to hire a clan warfare lawyer. What a pain in the ass.

But all that could wait.

I stood and walked over to Rainer. I was surprised to see Hutch in the basement. I'd never seen him or the rest of the crew arrive during the fight. He was already pulling the duct tape off Rainer's hands and feet. The crew had moved between the boy and the fight, blocking out the worst of the battle. My men had made sure my boy didn't see how awful things turned out. I was grateful for that. Rainer, now free, ran to me. He jumped into my arms, and I clung to him tightly, trying not to cry.

"I'm so sorry, buddy. I'm so sorry," I whispered fiercely.

"It's okay, Pop. I wasn't really scared. I knew you'd come for me."

His trust in me filled me with strength, and I hugged him tighter. Thankful that I had my son back, and he was safe.

Hutch was on the phone with Zo by the time we got upstairs. The rest of Chaos crew kept their distance, unsure what to do without their leader. Then, Hutch was telling the cops where to find them. Though, it sounded like they already knew. I heard sirens approaching. Someone had probably called when they started hearing gunshots.

Nearly three hours later, the report was filed with the Shifter Bureau and we were allowed to go home. Everything on our side was deemed self-defense and standard clan warfare. The long process of the night was over. Hutch drove Rainer and me back home.

It was almost dawn when we got back. The truck had barely come to a stop when the door burst open and Zo ran out. Rainer opened the door and ran to her.

"Mommy!" he yelled. I'd never heard him call her that.

Zoey was sobbing by the time he jumped into her arms. They hugged for a few moments before she pulled back to check on him. The rest of the crew we left behind to watch over her trickled out of the compound. Reck was with them. We hadn't trusted him to go with us.

He looked more relieved to see Rainer than any of them.

She saw the cut on Rain's head and his swollen, bruised eye. She didn't say anything at first, just picked him up and said he needed a bath. She walked past Reck and gave him a withering look that wilted my brother on the spot. The look on her face chilled me to the bone, and I knew I had one more thing to do before I could sleep for the next week straight. I waited until Zo was inside.

"Church! In the barn! Now!" I yelled.

"Now?" Hutch asked, beside me.

I nodded. "There's enough of us here to do it." Cars and bikes had started pulling in behind us. The rest of the crew were getting back home. We made our way to the barn. I walked with Reck. He looked terrified, but he'd made his bed.

I stood on a crate looking at the gathered crowd. Many were injured and tired, but none of them wanted to miss this.

"My brother, Trey Allen, has betrayed the Forest Heights clan. By his actions, he put my son, Rainer, in danger. He willfully consorted with a rival clan, and in so doing caused countless problems that we have had to sort out. I ask the clan, what should be done with Trey Allen?" I didn't use his nickname now, I didn't know if I ever would again.

"Cut his fucking balls off!" someone shouted. No laughter accompanied that.

"Twenty lashes!"

"Kick him out!"

"Yeah! Take his patch!"

"Take it!" The rest of the crowd started to shout.

The consensus sounded like it was what I'd planned all along. I stepped up to Trey, Hutch beside me.

I looked Trey in the eyes. "You'll always be my little brother, my family. But you don't really understand what brotherhood is. If you did, you'd have known that anyone in this crew would have killed for you, because they love you. It breaks my fucking heart that you didn't understand that. Maybe this is my fault." I shook my head. "Either way, you're done with the crew."

Trey's eyes filled with tears, but he didn't sob or beg. Instead, he just reached up to his jacket, took hold of his patch, and ripped it off the leather. He handed it to me. Then he turned away and left without a word.

As the sun started to come through the windows, I found Zoey in bed with Rainer. I didn't blame her. I didn't want the kid out of my sight, either. Zoey and Rainer were still awake, talking about baseball, of all things. We didn't push him to talk about what happened. I knew he'd been traumatized. We were just trying to let him know he was surrounded by love and safe now. He finally dozed off, snoring ever so faintly.

"I'll be to bed soon," Zoey whispered.

I nodded and leaned down and kissed Rainer on the head. I left, and somehow found the energy to take a shower, washing the blood, dirt and sweat off myself. I found Zoey just getting into bed when I came out of the bathroom.

"Is it really all over?" she asked me.

I told her what happened at the Chaos compound. I didn't leave out anything, knowing she'd want to know.

After I was done, she sighed and asked, "Are there any more enemies we need to worry about?"

"I honestly didn't know I had any until a few weeks ago. So, all I can say is, no, not that I know of."

She nodded, hopefully understanding. "Thank you for getting my baby back, Grizz."

"You guys mean more to me than anything. I would do anything for you. I am so sorry this happened, so damn sorry. I just hope you can forgive me for all this."

She lay on my chest then, and we both fell

asleep instantly.

Chapter 20 - Zo

Rainer stuck to me like glue for a couple of weeks after the... incident. Grizz and I talked about getting him into therapy, and we'd made an appointment with a shifter therapist connected to the club.

Grizz had been putting in major overtime, apologizing to me for not listening, apologizing to Rain for not being there to keep him from being taken. Rain had forgiven him, or rather hadn't ever held it against him. I'd forgiven him...for the most part. Every time I remembered the bruise on Rain's face, it was hard not to lash out at Rhett, at

Hutch, and especially at Reck, who hadn't been around much. The rage at the memory faded a little bit every day. I'd get past it, as long as nothing like this ever happened again. As the weeks wore on, I realized how much I missed Grizz. I'd been keeping him at arm's length.

It was time for that to stop.

That night, I ran a long bath, soaking, shaving, and taking my time. When I got out, I lotioned, spritzed, and plucked. By the time Grizz came in, I'd tucked myself into bed. "Hey," he said. "Sorry I'm so late. We had extra work at the shop today." He pulled off his boots and threw them into the closet. "I'm just going to take a shower."

He had no idea what I had planned. I smoothed out the blankets and turned out the light on my side of the bed. When he came to bed, I was all tucked in so he couldn't see what I had on underneath.

Nothing.

When he got under the covers, I scooted over, getting closer in the king-sized bed. That must've been enough for him to get the picture, because soon, it started. First the softest of touches against my skin. I could have ignored the first few as figments of my imagination, but the stroking grew stronger and more persistent against my side. Light, tickling touches that sent sparks of desire across my body.

I shifted to give Rhett better access to my body, letting the blanket fall to expose my breasts, my nipples already hardening at the thought of what was to come.

Mischief and happiness filled me, and keeping my eyes closed in the dim light from Rhett's side of the bed, I reached forward, smiling as I smoothed my palm across the hard planes of his chest. His nipples were already hard, and I leaned over to swirl my tongue around one.

He moaned softly as his hand tucked behind my neck. "Are you sure?" he whispered. "I don't want to rush you."

"I'm sure. Very sure. I think I want you to claim me tonight," I said, taking my mouth off of his nipple for a moment. He moaned when I went back to it.

I didn't have to wait long. Rhett reacted, pulling me on top of him so I straddled him. I laughed in delight when I realized he wasn't wearing anything, either.

Rhett drifted a feathery touch down the center of my back, right between my shoulder blades, to the top of my ass as he pressed his lips to my neck and my shoulder.

He sucked on my skin a little, pulling it between his teeth as small tendrils of pain snaked through me.

I pressed into him and moaned my pleasure, almost begging him to keep going. He began to knead my ass in firm strokes, encouraging me to rock back against him. When I did, his erection pressed against my wet core. We were both ready for the other.

Rhett moved his hands and ran them across my belly and down my thighs before dipping his thumb between my legs and stroking my clit. My muscles tensed at the sudden intense pleasure. I stiffened and then rolled my hips, creating a rhythm against his hand.

I moved against him, enjoying the stroke of a hand here and the nudge of his cock against my entrance until Rhett groaned. "I can't take much more."

I laughed as I opened my eyes. "Maybe you should learn to take things slower." I swung off of him, then took his hard cock in my hand in one fast movement. "Enjoy the experience."

He sucked in a long, hissing breath of pleasure and closed his eyes as he lifted his hips toward me. "I always enjoy experiences with you."

A wave of desire washed over me, and I wanted his touch against my skin and deep inside me. I rolled onto my back, and Rhett moved with me, palming one of my breasts. He dropped his lips to my collarbone and kissed up to my jaw. Rhett's soft hair tickled me as he moved, and he worked his way back down to suck my nipple into his mouth so he could tease it with his tongue until my hips lifted from the bed.

Rhett grabbed his cock, stroking it from base to tip in one smooth motion. I bit my lip as my clit pulsed with desire.

As I moaned, Rhett licked a scorching trail from my nipple to my hip, then across the top of my thigh. Sucking in my stomach, I held my breath in anticipation and parted my legs, inviting him to come, right where I needed him most. Where I was nearly about to combust.

"Please," I whispered. A prayer I knew he would answer. But he teased me by coming back to my mouth.

He growled, the deep rumbles like an erotic caress. I moaned again. He claimed my lips, and I opened my mouth to welcome his tongue, drawing it into my mouth and sliding it against mine, fighting to be closer, faster, and more passionate.

Rhett rested his palm on my belly, the touch heavy and warm, before drawing a finger up my slit to my clit.

"Fuck. You're so wet. But I can make you wetter." He waited just a moment before moving back down and replacing his finger with his tongue. He stroked it against me and dipped it just inside.

I squirmed and cried out, trying to find the right friction, trying to find my release, but he held me steady with his big, strong hands, remaining fully in control.

He licked and sucked until an orgasm broke over me, sending convulsions through me that started at my core and rocked out to my whole body.

I thrust my hands into Rhett's hair and pushed him closer so he couldn't move. "Don't stop. Don't you dare stop," I yelled out as he moved his hands to grip my hips, raising me to the perfect angle. I rode out the orgasm with Rhett sucking my clit until I finally relaxed against the bed.

As Rhett lifted himself above me again, his hard cock rubbed impatiently against my hip, and his hand jostled against me as he stroked it and cupped his balls. I reached for him and wrapped my fingers around it, before finding his rhythm.

He chuckled and I growled my displeasure at the change in his movements.

"Oh, you are demanding."

I nodded. "Yes, I am. Now, please lie down on your back."

A grin worked its way up his face, his teeth gleaming in the dim room. "Anything you ask, my mate." He chuckled again, and I sat up straight.

"On your back, or I'm taking matters into my own hands."

"Please do," Rhett muttered.

I grabbed his cock, taking the heavy weight into my hand, and he gasped as I drew him closer. As Rhett lay on the bed, his head resting on the pillows, I straddled the tops of his legs while everything inside me burned with the need to be satisfied by this man.

First, I teased him, drawing myself back and forth over his cock, smearing his precum over my core until he moaned and his fingers curled around my hips. He tried to pull me down to where he wanted me most.

I giggled and I stretched up, deliberately moving away. I ran my hands across Rhett's chest before I arched against him, my nipples brushing on his skin before I pulled his bottom lip into my mouth and bit down on it. He groaned, and I laughed again and wrapped my hand back around his cock, my touch light as I stroked him. I paid extra attention to the head, and his hips thrusted in my direction. Just once, but I backed right off. "I'm in control now."

I let him nudge against my entrance, and I held him there, in that perfect position of temptation.

My breathing slowed. We both held our breath and waited for me to move, lingering in that moment before everything became all about heat and sound and touch.

With no warning to Rhett, I pushed down hard and leaned forward, taking him into my body quickly and ever so satisfyingly.

"Fuck," Rhett gasped out, and he trailed his fingers down my spine as I rose back up.

He buried his hands in my hair, and I dug my fingers into his, both to hold him close and to stabilize myself for my next downward thrust onto his dick.

I changed my angle, moaning as I hit the perfect spot. Then again. And I just kept going, riding until neither of us could control our breathing, and I was no longer trying to control him.

Each movement I made sent a rush of electricity to spark across my nerves.

Rhett began to groan, in time with his breathing, and I sped up, bouncing on him faster and faster until he sat up and put his arms around me. "Now," I gasped as another, bigger, stronger orgasm burst over me.

Rhett opened his mouth and something inside transformed. His fangs lengthened, thick and large, too big for his mouth. I didn't have much time to get freaked out before he bit into my neck. There was a piercing pain for a moment, but soon it was replaced by the strongest orgasm I'd ever had. My entire groin area exploded, so hard I couldn't control anything. Not my mouth, not my body. Rhett and I writhed together, bonding in a magical, mystical way that could never be undone.

When the orgasm waned, he pulled his teeth back and when he smiled at me, the fangs were gone, and my love for him had intensified.

He didn't say a word, but his eyes shone with affection and devotion as he directed his gaze at me, and being watched whispered excitement through me as I rode him more, controlling his depth and angle to press against every part of me.

My thoughts began to scatter again until I could only move, driving myself up and down as Rhett's cock filled me and stretched me again and again and again. I didn't slow down. I didn't need to. Rhett rose to meet me, thrusting his cock harder and faster.

"Yes," he whispered. "Fuck, yes."

I dropped my hand between my legs, rolling my clit under my finger as Rhett moved in and out. Heat rose in my core, burning, turning me molten. This orgasm wasn't as potent as the last, but somehow it was sweeter. Was I feeling tendrils of Rhett's as well?

The tightness returned in my muscles, coiling each one until they almost ached. I screamed for release and then it hit. I held my breath, riding it out, not wanting the slightest movement to disturb it.

Beneath me, Rhett called my name as he thrust his hips one last time, pushing as far into me as he could, his balls pressed tight to my skin. His fingertips pushed into my hips, his grip tight enough to bruise as he held me still, each gasping breath he gave pumping another spurt of cum deep inside me.

I flopped forward, my head landing on his shoulder. "Holy Hell," I murmured. "We make quite the team."

We lay there for a while, basking in one another, until finally I rolled off of him and tucked myself into his side. "So now we're bonded," he whispered. "How do you feel?"

I smiled sleepily as I settled my hand over his torso. "Perfect. Like I was always meant to be here."

Rhett kissed the top of my head. "So you were."

Chapter 21 - Grizz

It'd been a full week since Rainer turned nine, and all he'd done was complain about his bones aching and his muscles being sore. I knew he was showing all the signs of his first shift.

I was so excited for him, but Zoey was freaking out with worry and really irritable.

She'd asked me about my first time about three weeks ago. I'd been a little too honest with her, explaining the process. It wasn't painful but it was disconcerting the first time.

Now she was like a mother hen, terrified her baby would get hurt. The full moon was coming on Friday, and I had no doubt it would be Rainer's first shift.

The night before the full moon, I was lying in bed when Zoey came in, climbed into bed, and straddled me. She looked out the window at the nearly full moon before leaning down and kissed me. "I love you so much, Grizz."

My heart still ached every time she said that. "I love you too, babe."

She licked her lips and sighed. "I need to tell you something."

"Uh-oh. That doesn't sound good," I said, only half-joking.

She ignored that. "There's more to my moodiness lately. It's not just Rainer getting ready to become a shifter. I didn't want to say anything, because...well, shit, I didn't think this could possibly happen again. But...my period is late, like really late."

My heart started to race, ready to explode out of my chest. I almost felt dizzy.

"All the mood swings and the late period, I went ahead and took a pregnancy test...three actually." She flushed dark red.

I was barely able to breathe, waiting for her to say what I already knew she was going to say.

"They were all positive. I'm pregnant, and I think it was the night you claimed me. I'm almost positive that was the night."

I rolled her over onto her back. She giggled as I did it, and I looked into her eyes. "Are you serious? Like, really, truly serious?"

She nodded at me, biting her lip. I still didn't understand how some humans could have shifter babies while others couldn't, though right then I didn't give a damn.

I smiled, genuinely thrilled. "I'm gonna be a daddy again! Oh, shit! I hope it's a girl! Then we can have one of each, a matching set like salt and pepper shakers. One that looks like me and one that looks like you."

Zoey laughed, looking relieved. My eyes welled up a little then, and I wiped at them.

"Are you okay?" she asked me.

"I just...I get to do it the right way this time. I don't have to miss so much. I missed so many things with Rainer, it still gets to me."

She put her hand on my cheek. "There is still going to be a ton of stuff to experience with Rainer. Like his first shift. Oh, and you have no idea how glad I am you get to have the birds and the bees and puberty talks with him instead of me having to do it. All this stuff we get to experience together."

"I love you so damn much, Zo."

"I love you too, Grizz."

The next night, I stood under the full moon behind the compound. Hutch had wanted to be there too, but I wanted it to be just the three of us.

He was with the rest of the crew about a hundred yards back, watching on. Even Reck was there, though he stood apart from the rest of the crew. Zoey was off to the left, wringing her hands nervously. Rainer stood next to me. I told him he didn't need to take his clothes off, so he stood next to me, grimacing. The shift was coming on strong. Even I could feel the pull of the moon. It had to have been bad for him.

Zoey had a look on her face like she wanted to stop all this, as if she could now. I shook my head at her to stay back. There was no way to stop the first shift, after that he would learn to control it, and do it on command.

"Rainer?" I said calmly. "Deep breaths. I know it's uncomfortable but—" Rainer fell to his knees and whimpered.

I held up a hand, keeping Zoey back. "I know it's uncomfortable, but you have to push it out of your mind. Your bear is in there, you just have to let him out. The reason it feels so weird is he's trapped and trying to get out. Once you let him out, everything will feel good again."

I knelt down and took my son's hands. Rainer looked up into my face with eyes full of tears, and his teeth were clenched together.

"Trust your bear, Rainer. Trust it, and this will stop."

Rainer bowed his head and took several deep shuddering breaths before looking back into my eyes.

"You are a fighter, Rainer. I'm so proud of everything you've overcome. I have never been more proud of anyone in my life. You are a fighter. Now prove it!"

Rainer smiled even through the shift. He stood and shouted, then yelled, growing louder every second. I heard it happen, the change in his voice. The yell got deeper, resonating even in my chest as the shout turned to a roar. Then, just like that, my boy was a bear. I heard the shouts from behind me as the clan cheered on the newest shifter. I turned around and saw Zoey crying, her hands to her face. I was surprised to see Reck just behind her, between us and the rest of the clan, his own look of pride evident on his face, tears streaming from his eyes too, smiling. My family was all here, and this was a glorious night.

I shifted and ran to Rainer. I nuzzled his face, letting him know how proud I was of him, then I took my boy on his first run.

Chapter 22 - Hutch

The beer in my hand was starting to go warm. I just didn't have a taste for it tonight. I was just putting on a show so nobody knew how bad I still felt.

I couldn't get over the fact that I let those sons of bitches take Rainer. I also should have seen what was going on with Reck. It had been weeks, and I was still mentally beating the shit out of myself.

The party was rowdy, everyone was stoked after watching Rainer shift for the first time. Hell, I'd been *beyond* excited. That hadn't lasted long though. For most of the night, I'd had a fake smile plastered on my face.

Zoey and Grizz hadn't held Rainer's abduction against me the way they had Reck, but I felt like there *had* to have been something more I could have done. It had all ended up okay, Rainer was over by the bonfire with a bunch of the other kids. He didn't look like anything at all had happened. It helped a little, knowing he was fine and safe, but not enough.

Suddenly my head was full of her smell, a combination of lilies, oranges, and the sweet scent of clean skin. Kim. I told myself not to look for her, but I still ended up letting my eyes dart around the crowd until I saw her round the corner of the house.

A White Claw in her hand, she was talking and laughing with one of the crew wives. She wasn't my typical girl. I'd always kind of gone for the blonde, porn star, bimbo types.

Kim was a beauty in a different way. A tight, athletic body, thick brown hair so dark it was almost black...there was just something about her. I'd been close to asking her out all those years ago, but then everything went down with Grizz and Zoey, and that had become an impossibility.

I nodded at her as she walked by, but she pretty much ignored me. I didn't have some complex where I needed women to notice me, to give me validation, but I couldn't get Kim out of my head. Being ignored did not help my mental space at all.

I must have let my facade slip a little, because a few minutes later a chick who was a regular around the compound came up to me and slid an arm around me. I was trying to remember her name. Tawny? Tammy? Teresa?

She whispered in my ear. "You look like you need some help getting out of that funk, big guy."

I chuckled without humor. "I'm fine, no big deal."

She slid a finger across my chest and said, "Oh, come on! When's the last time you got laid? I'd love to put a smile on that handsome face."

I sighed. I wasn't really in the mood, hadn't

been for a few weeks, but it *had* been a while.

Maybe a little roll in the hay would get my mind

off everything else. I was about to accept her

offer, when I heard an engine screaming up the

driveway. Whoever it was had the car going faster

than anyone should have been going. They

slammed on the brakes, sliding nearly ten feet

through the gravel, and a giant of a man leapt

from the car. The dude was fucking huge, almost

as big as Grizz.

"You bitch! You thought you could hide

from me!"

I thought he was yelling at one of the crew

groupies or something then I saw him walking

straight toward Kim, *what the fuck?* I disentangled myself from the girl and made my way cautiously forward. Kim looked like she'd *literally* seen a ghost, a look of fear and horror on her face.

The guy was still walking toward her, the party was dead silent, and no one knew what the hell was happening.

He pointed at her and screamed, "You think you can just dump me? Take my money and leave?"

I didn't know what the hell was happening, but I was *not* letting this guy get to her. He looked ready to kill. I walked faster, pushing through the crowd.

"Fucking whore! Are you up here fucking some goddamn mongrel bears? Just like a whore! Come here!"

He was raising his hand to strike Kim, and she was raising her arms to fend him off, her legs about to buckle in fear. I burst forward, staying human, but letting my bear speed and strength take over.

I snatched his hand just as it swung toward her face. I let his momentum do most of the work, and twisted his arm around behind his back. Once it was locked in place, I grabbed his wrist and twisted it.

There was a snap like a dead tree branch breaking. Before he could scream in pain, I snapped my leg up, and the toe of my boot slammed into his temple. His face crashed into the gravel, unconscious.

Kim stared down at the mountain of muscle that lay at our feet. She looked shocked and relieved all at once. She finally glanced up at me, her blue eyes locking onto mine, and my heart fluttered.

"Thank you!" she whispered.

I shrugged. "No problem. Who the hell is this guy anyway?" I asked.

She ran a hand through her hair and sighed. "My piece-of-shit ex-husband."

Made in the USA
Monee, IL
01 September 2023

41974888R00298